INTRUDERS: INVASION

INTRUDERS BOOK 1

TRACY SHARP

ONE

The first sign that the world was ending was disturbing, but not alarming. It was insidious, because it was disguised as an everyday kind of horror. Something that, although terrible, had become almost commonplace in our world. Things like this happened every day, somewhere. All you had to do was watch the news to see evidence of horrible, but not shocking (not anymore) things people do to one another on a daily basis.

It started with the disappearances. Babies and children vanishing from their beds. First one, then another. And another. Until it did become alarming. By the time we knew something odd was happening, the invasion was well underway.

People were comfortable in the belief that we were safe. That everything would be all right. That the world would go on, continue as it always had, one donut shop paper cup of coffee at a time. We were smug and oblivious; a combination which made the invasion inevitable and rapid.

We were easy pickings.

But then, I doubt there would be much anyone could've done, anyway.

Our militaries were no match for them.

Nothing was.

ONE OF THE first to vanish was my niece, Jessica. She was two years old. Almost three. I was in the house when it happened because I lived with my sister, Kelly.

Which is why I was sitting at the police station right now, being questioned by the cops.

"Tell me again what happened that night, Zoe." The cop was older. He had a kind face. Most would call him fatherly. He spoke to me in soft, gentle tones. "How did you get the shiner?"

I shrugged, which is what I'd done the last several times he asked me. "I was in a fight with some girl at the college. She spit at me. I hit her. She hit me back. End of story."

"That sucks. You've had a rough couple of days."

I shrugged. Nodded.

"Start from the beginning, Zoe. Okay?" His voice was so gentle. It made me uncomfortable.

So although I was tired and annoyed because I'd been sitting there for hours, his kindness was disarming. I pushed out a breath and started again. But I skipped the good parts.

"I'd just gotten home from work. Kelly asked me if I'd watch Jessica for a couple of hours so they could go out for a bite. He'd received a Christmas bonus from work, and wanted to celebrate."

The cop, Detective Elliot Rayback, leaned forward, his hands slowly turning his Styrofoam cup on the table. "What time did they leave?"

"Around seven-thirty."

"You work at the college, you said, right?" He was trying to confuse me, by jumping back and forth in the story. A technique that often works if a suspect is lying.

"Yes."

"And you drove home?"

"Yes."

"At what time?"

"Eight. I stood around watching the meteor for a while." A small meteor had crashed on top of the physical education building at the campus. It was something I definitely hadn't expected when I got up that morning.

"Yeah, that was something else, wasn't it?"

Indeed it was. If he only knew. I nodded.

"Right in our little town." He shook his head. His tone was friendly and conversational, like he was talking to someone he'd known and liked forever.

"Did you get pictures? Like on your phone?"

I shook my head. "Too freaked out."

He chuckled. "I bet you were."

I wanted to offer him a smile but I couldn't make my face do it. My nerves were jangling.

"Anyway, it was snowing, right?"

"Yeah."

"That snow makes the roads slippery. Treacherous. Believe me, I've seen my share of car fatalities because of weather. People just aren't as careful as they should be. They think they're immortal or something."

This time I did offer a tiny smile, and was amazed I could manage it. I was so tired. My neck and shoulders ached from sitting there so long. My back screamed. Grief sat in my belly like a rock. "Can I stand up for a while?"

"Sure, Zoe. Stretch yourself out." Detective Rayback

kept his demeanor calm and laid back, but his eyes casually watched every single thing about me.

"Thanks." I stood, stretching, my red combat boots creaking a little.

Rayback took in the boots, the worn, straight legged jeans rolled up to the ankles; a style made popular by the punks of the seventies and eighties. I wore my black The Clash t-shirt worn over a long sleeved black tee; the t-shirt I found in a box of memorabilia Kelly and I went through after the death of our mother.

"I remember The Clash. I actually went to see them in New York city back when they were big. Great show. Joe Strummer was a serious musician. Not everyone knows that, you know."

I nodded, letting him know I was listening. But skin was crawling beneath my scalp.

"I like your hair, Zoe. Very cool. The black hair with the red streaks catches the eye. Cool cut, too."

"Thanks. A friend at Antonio's did it for me."

"The hairdressing school?"

I nodded. This was all wrong. I shouldn't even be here. I didn't understand how this all happened. And beneath this, a gnawing, tearing panic. My niece was missing. Someone snatched her, right under my nose.

"That's an expensive hairstyling school. My wife's sister went there. How did you come up with the cash for that?"

Anger shot through me. Of course he was suggesting I stole it. Hadn't I been in trouble with the law for stealing before?

The truth was more shameful to me than if I'd been a real thief. I'd stolen a loaf of bread at fourteen; went to court mandated counseling and mom went to AA meetings. They'd taken it easy on me.

"My mother had a life insurance policy." It was for a hundred grand, which my sister and I split, and which allowed me to enroll in the hairstyling school in Saratoga. Rayback was right. It was the best hairstyling school in the area. I couldn't have afforded to go there if it hadn't been for the policy.

"Right. I'm sorry about your mother, Zoe." His voice softened. He must've read something in my face. Maybe that I wasn't happy my mother was dead.

But I was relieved. I was ashamed for it, but there is was. She'd been a hardcore drunk for a lot of years, and anyone who has an alcoholic for a parent knows what that means.

In the end, Kelly and I had to keep scooping Mom off the street, where she'd inevitably passed out; many times outside of a bar. She'd fall asleep in her car if she was lucky. She'd ended up in the hospital more times than I could count in the last few years.

I took a few breaths to try to keep myself from sobbing, but felt my chin as it began to tremble.

Detective Rayback's gaze stayed on my face, the wheels in his brain turning. I was betting he thought I was wracked with guilt because I had something to do with Jessica's disappearance.

Telling him I didn't was pointless. I've already told him this, many times. But everyone who ended up in this room likely denied any guilt or wrongdoing.

So Rayback said nothing as I slowly walked the length of the small room used for questioning suspects. I noticed the double-sided mirror the moment I walked in. The place was more like the movies than I'd thought.

His silence was unnerving. I preferred the endless questions. I could see why cops used it. It would make someone who was guilty nervous because you wouldn't know what the cop was thinking. But it made me nervous too, even though I had nothing to do with Jessica's vanishing.

I stopped and took a deep, shuddering breath. I turned to look at him. I imagined what he saw when he looked at me: a young girl who was full of anger; whose mother drank herself to death; literally and who had been in trouble with the law already, for stealing. So although I knew it wouldn't do any good, I looked at him through tear blurred eyes and said, "I didn't hurt Jessica. I had nothing to do with this. I love her."

"Okay, Zoe," Rayback said. "But I need to hear it again. Kelly and Derek are home when you get there."

I turned my eyes heavenward and continued to walk the room, pacing. It was what trapped animals do, and I felt trapped --- Exhausted, heartsick and trapped. "Yes."

"What kind of mood were they in, Zoe?"

"Great. Derek got a five hundred dollar Christmas bonus from work. He was taking her out to celebrate and he gave me twenty bucks to order a pizza."

"You left that part out," Rayback said.

"Well, he did. And so I ordered a medium pepperoni and cheese and the box with the remaining half was on the table when you guys showed up." Frustration edged my tone. What the hell did it matter if I left out the pizza?

"It isn't easy being an eighteen year old with a baby." Rayback's steady gaze stayed on my face.

"No. It isn't. That's why I moved in with Derek and Kelly, to help out. With us toggling our shifts, there would always be someone home to watch Jessica."

"It helped you out, too, right? How much did they charge you for rent?"

"Just a hundred bucks a month, and I helped with groceries."

"That was for room and board, basically, right? Where was the room?"

I sighed. This again. He knew where the room was. Right next to Jessica's room. In fact, if Jessica woke up in the night, I heard her first. The baby monitor was in my room, because neither Kelly or Derek heard her crying. They both slept like the dead. "Right next to Jessica's room."

"Right. Right. You got up with her more than anyone."

"Yes. I'm a light sleeper. Derek and Jessica could both sleep through an earthquake."

"Good thing you moved in, then, huh?" His gaze stayed on my face, watching for a the slightest reaction.

I nodded. "I'm sure they're not the first parents to not wake up when their kid cries."

"How old are you, Zoe?" He knew the answer to that question.

I tried not to grit my teeth. "Seventeen."

"That's mighty young to be caring for a baby."

I shrugged. "Lots of people do it. And it's not all the time."

He paused, and the silence stretched out for what seemed like forever.

I knew Kelly and Derek were also being questioned in rooms just like this one, just in case we were all involved in Jessica's disappearance. Accidents happened. People lost control of themselves sometimes.

"You and Kelly are pretty close, aren't you?"

I nod. "We had to be."

"It's tough having a mother who drinks."

I said nothing. What was there to say? Having a mother

who drinks means you really have no mother. You are the parent --- of yourself, your siblings and your mother.

He clearly knew this. Cops deal with all kind of people. What people are capable of doing when they don't have the mental resources to parent, because they had piss poor parents, and don't know how. He's also seen what people will do to protect someone.

But I turned out the opposite. I was an excellent aunt to Jessica. I catered to her every need, before she even needed it.

Kelly? She wasn't terrible. But she relied on me a lot to take care of Jessica. Because it came naturally to me. Which was a joke. If you saw me, you'd know why. I don't exactly look like the warm, fuzzy kind. But people will surprise you. I surprised myself.

"What happened then?"

"I ate pizza. Fell asleep on the couch until they came home."

"And then?"

"Kelly and Derek went to peek in on Jessica."

He said nothing, still watching me. Waiting for me to go on.

"And she wasn't there. She was gone."

RAYBACK LEFT me alone for a while. I was sure he and other cops were watching my every move behind the two-way mirror. I'd been there so long, and I was so tired, I just stared at the table like a zombie. They wouldn't let me sleep.

If I closed my eyes, someone would walk in with coffee

or a soda, or ask if I needed anything. They make sure I stayed awake.

I leaned forward and placed my head in my hands, scratching at my scalp. It felt like my skin was crawling. Were they even looking for Jessica?

Panic made my adrenaline spike, and for a moment I thought I'd hyperventilate. *I must look guilty as hell.*

I needed to get out of here. Jessica needed me. I had to find her.

I thought of yesterday, before this happened. How much life had changed since then.

THE LIGHTS HAD STILL BEEN on at the Ripley College education building when I pulled into the parking lot. I went to the hairstyling school in Saratoga Springs during the day, and I cleaned at night. The college is on the outskirts of Ripley, the town where I live.

The temperature seemed to have dropped ten degrees from when I started the drive a mere twenty minutes before. The chill air hitting my face made my breath catch in my throat. It actually hurt to take a breath. The cold snap had started a few days ago and it seemed like it had been going on forever. Especially for someone whose car heater doesn't work.

The old combat boots I'd snagged at the thrift store downtown were awesome, but they didn't do much to keep my feet warm. Of course, having socks full of quickly expanding holes didn't help either. I'd have to invest in warmer socks and boots soon. The boots I'd get from the thrift store, if I didn't find them on clearance somewhere, but the socks I refused to buy second hand. So I'd have to pinch pennies for those. Hard to do when you have so few pennies to pinch. I had to make the little bit of money left from my mother's policy last. But at least I'd landed an internship at Make the Cut, the salon downtown. I was to start the following Sunday full-time, and it was two days away.

The heat of the school felt wonderful when I first stepped through the doors, but soon felt stifling. Some parts of the college had the heat blasting, while other parts were frigid. I'd learned every corner of the place during my year cleaning for Joe.

Moving quickly, I made my way to the women's locker room, just outside the exercise room and pool. I wasn't scheduled to work, and I didn't plan on going back to the college after this night. But I had a score to settle.

"Let's see what we can find today, shall we?" I said to the lock as I held it to my ear and slowly turned the dial. It didn't take long to hear the first click. Another twenty seconds and I heard the second. The third took about a minute, and I was starting to sweat. I like to be quick when I'm breaking into lockers. It's better that way.

I used to do it for the thrill of getting away with it. But since Jessica was born, I'd turned over a new leaf. She deserved better than a thief for an aunt.

The particular locker I was breaking into now belonged to a tall cheerleader type who'd tossed a gum wrapped on the floor in front of me as I was sweeping the floor. Later on, after her class and while I was mopping, she spit her gum right on top of the mop. The mop was an old fashioned jobbie with all the strings.

Messy.

The woman's locker room --- as much a joy for me now

as it had been in high school. Ah, nostalgia. Nice to know that the bitches of my gender never change.

I'd endured jabs about the red and purple streaks in my black hair. I'd endured the jabs about my less than fashionable clothes (according to the fashion squad). I'd even endured the snickers about my worn combat boots.

But gum on my mop?

Well now, that was a horse of a different color. I was pissed.

I looked up at her and met her sneer with one of my own. I knew where her locker was because she walked to it every second day before and after her 7:00 p.m swim class. And I just happen to have a flare for picking locks of all kinds.

Call it a talent, maybe even a calling.

Really, though, it was just a hobby. I did it for the challenge, and never actually stole what I found behind the locks.

Anyway, she shoved her purse, $800 android phone and Gucci handbag complete with matching Gucci wallet, credit cards, and cash in there.

The lock popped open and I smiled like a kid at Christmas. I quickly removed it and opened the locker. There was my booty.

"Hello, my lovelies." I removed everything from her locker and shoved it into my backpack, including the lock. Then I high tailed it out of there. As my old combats clicked on the freshly washed floor, I hummed a merry tune.

Yup. That had been one expensive wad of gum. I hoped she'd enjoyed it before horking it at my mop.

Was I afraid of getting caught? Nope. No one here knew my real name. Joe paid me under the table. Luckily for me, it was just how he did things. I wouldn't be back here.

I pushed through the side door leading to the back staircase, as I didn't think that using the main stairs or elevator would be prudent at this time.

I took the stairs two at a time and jumped the last five to the bottom, then ripped the door at the bottom open and quickly booted it down the hall. I was almost to the back door of the first floor when a voice made me jump.

"Hey!"

I spun around on my heel, wondering what I'd do if it was campus security. Giving up wasn't an option. They'd take me to the cop shop no matter what. So I prepared to run.

Three guys were at the other end of the hall. These three I'd seen before, leering at me and chuckling in the cafeteria as I'd washed the floors. No doubt they were watching my ass. You keep pretty trim just eating packages of crackers you pocketed from the kitchen, while the more wealthy college students chowed down on steak sandwiches or pizza. The smells of which are heavenly.

But I told myself I didn't like that crap anyway, as my stomach growled over and over again.

The middle one, the one I'd already pegged as the alpha of the bunch, lifted his chin expectedly at me. His hair was perfect, and had more product in it than I'd ever seen on a girl's hair. The other two snickered, chins down, glancing at each other in anticipation.

This wasn't good. Not even a little.

I was in an empty lower hallway that was rarely used. They must've spotted me walking through here before, and waited for me at the other, darker end. I hadn't seen them.

Engaging them would seem like an invitation no matter

what I said, because when you say anything, you open up the lines of communication. So even 'piss off, jackwad' can sound like, 'hey, big boy, come talk to me' to the narcissist.

So instead I spun on my heels and quickened my pace. I was only about forty feet from the door.

"Hey! Raggedy Ann! I'm talking to you! Want to make some money? I know you can use the cash. It'll be real easy."

I rolled my eyes and walked even faster. Thirty feet.

"HEY!" The sound of footfalls running.

I didn't need to turn around to know they were now full out chasing me, and their intensions were not honorable.

But I'm a fast runner. It comes from running in the dead of night when creepy guys suddenly appear behind me when my car is dead, again, and I miss the last bus out of this place.

Blasting through the door, I ran full-tilt across the slick, icy walkway leading to the back end of the building, skidding and falling on my knees. They were on me in a second. If one fell, there were two others to grab me. Not many people around at this time of the night in the early winter. None were at the back of the building. The parking area was empty. My idea was to lay low and take the wooded walkway to the main parking lot where my car was parked.

But now I was alone with three assholes who wanted to take something from me that I wasn't willing to give. Not while I was alive, anyway.

Maybe that didn't matter to them.

They could pretty much do what they wanted to me if they got a good hold on me.

"Get her behind those trees!" The leader of the pack grunted. Excitement quickened his tone. His breaths were coming quick and ragged. He'd been thinking about this for some time, apparently.

One grabbed my wrists while the other two each grabbed a leg, and I screamed my lungs out, kicking and flailing to no avail. I'm a small girl. I weigh a hundred and five pounds after a big meal, which is rare. I have a wicked fast metabolism so I burn fat before it has a chance to settle.

I couldn't believe this was actually happening to me. Campus rapes happen all the time. Usually, though, the girl is drunk and never reports it. They're too ashamed and know the blame will be shifted to them. They can't remember if they were *too flirtatious* or not, like it mattered.

I screamed my throat raw. But nobody was around to hear it. The last classes of the night haven't let out yet.

I screamed again and got a punch in the face for my trouble. They dropped me in a thick copse of trees and I could see the sky between their heads. Slow, fat snowflakes were falling on my face. In my eyes and mouth. I felt hot and cold at the same time. The trees loomed above me, branches frosted in snow. The scene would be gorgeous if I wasn't about to be raped and beaten. This was the wooded area around a long bike path which snaked through the college grounds. Great also for jogging.

Nobody was jogging now.

The leader smiled down at me, his face already flushed with arousal. "Look, Raggedy Ann. This is happening to you whether you like it or not. So shut the fuck up."

"Don't fight and it'll be over quicker," one of the other guys said.

The third stayed quiet, he stood back a little, like the reality of what they were about to do to me was sinking in, and it scared him.

I locked eyes with him. "Please."

He took a step toward me, but stopped. He shook his head, his own eyes panicked. Like the actions unfolding before him had already been set in motion and there was nothing he could do about it.

He'd been involved up to now. He'd helped carry me there. He was into it up to his eyeballs.

Still, I tried again, but it came out as a croak. "Please."

And amazingly, it seemed to work. The guy stammered, "Jordan. Maybe we shouldn't—"

But Jordan already had his jeans shoved down, and was kneeling between my legs when he said, "Shut up and don't be a pussy. Hold her legs."

The other friend giggled as he knelt on my wrists, keeping me from fighting back.

But then, like some kind of gift from the gods, I looked up and saw a ball of fire in the sky, blasting down toward us, sizzling and sparking, crackling as it lit up the heavens.

Everything stopped.

"Holy shit!" The giggler shouted, and pushed himself back, standing up.

That left my hands free. While Jordan looked up, I brought my knee back and booted him in the throat. I heard a crunch. He clawed at his throat and choked, making gasping, gurgling sounds.

I tugged my jeans back up while the other two continued to gawk at the thing in the sky.

Taking the opportunity fate had gifted to me, I slid my boot knife from my combat and stepped forward, slicing the giggler's face. He turned to me, eyes wide with shock. I grinned, waving the knife around in front of me, murder in my eyes.

"Crazy bitch," he sputtered, blood spilling between the fingers pressed to the gash in his cheek.

"Yeah, that's right." I smiled widely. "Go call a cop."

He did a comical little skipping move before he tapped his friend on the arm. "Let's go."

The friend, who had made the feeble attempt to stop my attack, looked at me, shame crossing his face, and followed his buddy toward the main parking lot.

I kept hold of the boot knife in case there were any other creeps lurking with the same idea these guys had, looking up at the fire streaking down from the sky as it rocketed toward us.

It landed with a huge crash, sounding like a bomb in slow motion.

Heat radiated toward me, and my hair blew backward as a burning wind swept over me.

I said a silent prayer of thanks as I made my way toward the landing site, which amazingly, happened to be through the top of the Physical Education building, housing the gym and pool, and locker that I'd just robbed.

EVERYTHING HAD a dreamlike quality as I made my way to the PE building. There was a grayish, silvery dust floating through the air, coating everything around it. The dust was being dispersed by the wind, landing in trees and sailing through the air with the wet snow that fell through it. The smell was sulfuric, and some of the powder landed on my lashes. I blinked it away. Wet snow dribbled over my cheeks, chilling me. I began to shiver, despite the heat radiating from the crash site and the steaming ground near my feet.

Pockets of steam popped and whistled upward, like a

pot of boiling sauce. I looked down at the ground, watching as if hypnotized. The scene before me was surreal.

Heat radiated from the PE building. The snow had melted all around it, and bubbled at my feet. I stood just on the periphery of it, stopping just before the sizzling, popping heat on the ground.

The building was coated in the dust, the ground around it dotted with glowing embers of various sizes and shapes. A fire had started in the ceiling where the thing had landed.

A bespeckled kid walked toward me, his eyes round behind his Harry Potter glasses. "It's a meteorite. I can't believe it. Have you ever seen anything like this?"

I shook my head. "No."

"This is incredible!" He held up his phone, recording the flaming, smoking, dust covered site as the sirens screamed toward us. He smiled at me, his face awestruck, then pointed his phone toward me. "We're witness to an historical happening right now. What's your name?"

"Zoe." I saw my reflection in the screen of his phone, and blinked at what I saw. The wild, disheveled girl that looked back had dodged a bullet because of the meteorite.

But many others died because of it.

The fall-out of the crash hadn't yet begun.

At that point, I couldn't help but be thankful for it. I revelled in the dust falling all around me.

TWO

Finally, I was released from questioning. Rayback insisted on driving me home. My sister and Derek were still at the station being questioned.

The events of the last twenty-four hours had been so unbelievable, I wondered if I'd been hallucinating. I hoped that I had.

Rayback's car was cold at first, and I ducked down into the seat, my thrift store army issued jacket rising around my jaw. The winter hat on my head was another find from my mother's things. A pink and grey, whimsical thing with an exaggerated pom-pom on the top. It was far too cheerful for me, but it was hers, and strands of her chestnut hair were still woven into the yarn.

I didn't know why I felt like I needed her things near me. Little snatches of her with me, at all times. I guess I remembered the mother she was when Kelly and I were little --- before the drink took over.

The thing I remembered most was her smile. The wide, lovely smile that lit up her entire face. I remembered her wearing this hat, outside in the snow, making snow angels with her two small daughters.

I held on to that memory with a death grip, because it was the thing that reminded me that my mother had loved me at one time.

"Zoe, if you know something, you need to tell me. If you're trying to protect Kelly or Derek, you're not doing them any favors."

I stared straight ahead, through the windshield at the falling snow. The wipers moved back and forth steadily, making me feel sleepy. I felt so tired, and knew that if I closed my eyes right then, I'd nod off without a problem.

"Do you know where Jessica is, Zoe?"

His words snapped me back to reality. I turned to him and stared. "No. I wish I did. But I'm . . ."

He watched me, and his eyes were a strange mix of expectation and compassion. "You're what, Zoe?"

The words stuck in my throat. I could barely get them out, because if I did, it would make it real. I whispered them. "I'm so scared."

"Of what? Tell me, what are you scared of?"

I'd been scared when the three guys had attacked me at the college. But this kind of fear was real. It was a raw, intense fear that made it hard for me to even think. It paralyzed me. Jessica was gone. Someone had her. Was she being cared for? Was she cold? Hungry? Scared? Was she still alive?

A sob caught in my throat, making me swallow. My breath hitched. Again, I whispered, because what I was telling him was too horrible to say out loud. "That she's dead."

I regretted the words as soon as they were out of my mouth. It would just give Rayback something to grab on to.

He'd misunderstand what I was trying to say. It was fear. Fear. Not guilt. What else could you think when a two year old is stolen from her bed?

"After three hours, the odds of finding an abducted child alive drop drastically, don't they?" I asked him.

Rayback opened his mouth to say something but his cell chirped. It must've been important because even though I could tell he wanted to ignore it, he lifted the cell to his ear. "Yeah."

I took deep breaths to try to calm the rising panic threatening to choke me. It was the most helpless feeling in the world, having a child you love taken from you and not being able to do anything about it. A scream began to bubble up in my throat and I swallowed it down. Hysteria threatened to send me into a shrieking fit.

I opened the passenger door and almost fell out of the car. My combats sank into slush, and I felt icy water seeping through to my socks. The freezing air puffed out from my mouth as I took gulps of breath into my lungs, trying to stop the rush of dread from taking over.

Where is she? Who would've taken her?

This isn't the best neighborhood. I checked her windows, they were locked from the inside. The locks were not broken.

Could someone have picked the front or back door lock and snuck past me while I slept on the couch?

But Kelly and Derek had to use their key to get in, and the doors were both locked.

They could've locked the door on the way out, with Jessica.

But we'd been through this, over and over, Rayback and me. It sounded ridiculous even to me. Unbelievable. But there was no other answer.

Do you sleep walk, Zoe? He'd asked me.

No. But I used to as a kid. I left that part out. Still, I'd never hurt Jessica. She was the best thing in my life. I'd take a bullet for her. I'd---

"Zoe."

Rayback's voice steadied me, and I turned to look at him.

He stood at the cruiser, slammed the car door and walked toward me, his face serious. As he approached, his eyes skipped over me.

I hesitated on my feet, still standing in several inches of slush, water seeping through my boots.

I dropped my gaze and looked down at myself. I was a mess. Inside and out. I pulled my eyes back up to his.

He had news. And it wasn't good.

My stomach knotted, my bladder loosening, about to let go. A faint tremble moved over my body. My teeth began to chatter as my legs grew rubbery. *Please, please don't let her be dead.*

I looked up at him, waiting, unable to even breathe.

"There have been more disappearances." His was face was a study in bafflement.

I frowned, not sure I understood what he was telling me. "How many? In Ripley?"

He shook his head. "Thousands. All over the world."

THOUSANDS OF BABIES AND CHILDREN, from newborns to ten years old, gone. Vanished overnight, without a trace.

"What in hell is going on?" I sat watching the news. It

was on every single station. No one could explain it. The children were just gone.

Then came scenes of meteor crashes all over the globe. The crash at the college had only been one of thousands. Entire cities were coated in dust.

Of course they had to be connected. But the implications of what I was seeing flicker madly across the TV screen was too crazy to wrap my mind around.

Crazy things were happening. People were going insane, running the streets. News reports showed scene after scene of people locking their jaws around someone's arm, throat, or face, blood spurting into the air and coating them. People were sending in phone recordings.

It was happening all over the planet. The entire world had gone insane. In a single night. I could still smell the remnants of the meteor dust in my hair and on my jeans. It had gotten into my eyes, and seeped into my pores. Would I turn out like those lunatic people on TV?

I booted up my laptop and tried to search the cause of the bizarre, lunatic behavior people were displaying all over the world. What was making them go so crazy?

Report after report suggested that it had been something in the meteor dust. Not everyone seemed to be affected in the same way. The reason why some people were going insane and others weren't seemed to be a complete question mark.

But then I found it. A real time recording on PheedMe made by a kid of about fifteen years old. He was using a webcam, and kept looking away, nervously toward some source of noise off to his left.

"If anybody is watching this, It's eight o'clock, December 10th, two-thousand fourteen."

A chill crept over me. He looked terrified.

"I know why people are biting. They aren't alive. They're dead." He sobbed. Wiped tears from his eyes with his forearm. "My dad died of a heart attack a half hour ago."

Banging and screaming from off to his left. The kid looked toward the noise, his face frightened. "I was helping my mom cover him up. He got up. Teeth snapping at me. Grabbing for me. He got my mother. She hasn't gotten up yet but I don't think it'll be long. I've locked them both in their room."

My mouth dropped open. I stared at the screen.

"I'm waiting for someone to come and help me! The dead are everywhere outside. Banging on the windows. Wandering around the streets. They are killing people and making more like them, because when you die, you come back . . . like that. If you can get to me, if you have a gun, I'm at 3 Pinewood Ave in Ripley. Please, help me. I don't know how much longer that door will hold."

He'd kept his webcam on, but he was out of the screen shot now. I waited, watching for him. Stunned.

Rayback had taken off after making sure I was okay. That had been about a half hour ago.

I thought of Jessica. Maybe it was better that she wasn't here right now. I hoped that wherever she was, it was safer than here.

I KEPT WATCHING the kid's video, then getting up and peering between the blinds into the streets. There was nothing moving out there. I wondered if I should try to go out and stock up on food for when Kelly and Derek came home. And for when Jessica came home, if she ever did. From the warnings on the news that everyone should stay inside until the situation was controlled, it might be a while before we could get out there again.

The kid hadn't made another appearance on his webcam. I hoped that someone had rescued him. How many other kids were out there, waiting for help? How many was it too late for?

Stop. One thing at a time. I tried to think through the hysteria threatening to take over. I couldn't help the nagging feeling of urgency. The feeling that I had to move; to do something.

But what if Jessica came back?

It was a crazy thought, but she had vanished inexplicably. Maybe she would reappear the same way.

If nobody was here, then she'd be alone. A two year old toddling around, looking for me or for her parents. I couldn't bear the thought that she'd be crying and scared, and completely alone.

So I stayed. I kept surfing the web, going back to the kid's video.

Then I bundled up in a blanket on the couch and stared at the TV, waiting for something to happen. Waiting for some sign that the insanity was being controlled; that normalcy would be restored.

But in the back of my mind, I knew it never would be. Not with Jessica gone.

And not with the dead getting up and eating people.

This can't be happening. It can't be happening.

The news confirmed it. The dead were rising. If anyone had a dead person in their house, they should leave, or get the dead out. Someone would collect them when they could get to them.

That was the advice people were getting from the news.

Connected to the meteor dust.

The president called for military action.

I barked out a laugh. "Yeah. I guess he did. Smart move."

Numbness spread over me and I let out a long, hysterical laugh, the sound of it wild and unhinged.

I couldn't believe what I was seeing. What I was hearing.

I hadn't slept in over twenty-four hours, and the shock had wiped me out. The adrenaline had been racing through my veins for so long that when I finally calmed down a little, trying to think things through, the absence of the adrenalin spikes left me exhausted.

I didn't even realize it when my eyes closed.

"Doe-doe!"

I kept my eyes closed because I thought I was dreaming. I heard Jessica's voice calling me. She always called me Doe-doe because she couldn't say Zoe yet.

"Doe-doe-doe-doe!" This time the word was accompanied by a light pat on my face.

My eyes snapped open and a cry escaped me. There she was; standing in front of the couch, a big grin on her face. Her red curls had turned white blonde, and her blue eyes were now green, but it was definitely Jessica. And she seemed happy and perfect.

"Jessie!" I sat up and scooped her up into my arms, hugging as hard as I dared, afraid to hurt her. "Where have you been?"

"Seeping. I woked up!"

"I see that! Did you have a good sleep?" I sat back and looked into her now strangely pale green eyes.

She nodded. She held her white stuffed cat by the neck. "Kitty!"

"Kitty had a good sleep, too?"

Jessica nodded again, her blonde ringlets bouncing.

Where the hell had she been? Where ever it was, she had no memory of it or of who took her.

"Where mommy?" Jessie asked me.

"I'm going to see if I can get her home. Okay? Are you hungry?"

Jessie nodded. "Nana."

"One banana coming up." I found Netflix for her and put a children's movie on. She didn't need to be seeing what was happening in the world outside. Dread crept over me. How was I going to keep her safe with what was going on out there?

I found a banana for her on the counter, which was a day away from being too ripe. Peeled it and cut it up into bites-sized pieces and tossed them in one of her little plastic bowls with cute little ducks on them. I went back into the living room and placed the bowl between her chubby little legs.

"Milk?" she grabbed a slice of banana in one hand and mashed it into her mouth. While chewing she managed a gooey, "Pease?"

"Of course!" I grabbed a sippy cup from the cupboard and poured milk into it. We were getting low. Jesus. How the hell would I get her the things she needed with this chaos going on? It wasn't like I could take a little jaunt to the corner store.

After giving Jessie her milk I left her happily giggling at the cartoon and stepped back into the kitchen. I used my cell to dial the number Rayback had given me. There was no answer. I left a message on his cell phone, letting him know that Jessie had reappeared and was safe. I left out the part about her hair and eye color changing. Right now it was the least of our problems.

Next, I called the police station. Nobody answered there, either. Ditto for Derek and Kelly's cell phones.

I looked at my cell, frustrated, then froze.

The date on the screen said Dec 12th. I'd slept through the night and day, and it was now night time again. 7:10, to be exact.

Suddenly the pressure in my bladder was terrible. I couldn't believe I'd held it that long.

Jessie was still happy as could be; eating bananas and watching a cartoon alien shoot and disintegrate a cartoon dog on the TV screen.

As I emptied my bladder, I tried to make sense of what the hell was going on. Why had I slept so long? Was the world in any better shape since I'd drifted off?

I washed my hands and headed back into the kitchen to check news reports on the laptop.

Before I sat down at the laptop, I looked out the living room window. There were shapes wandering the streets now; shambling. This wasn't a normal walk. It was dark, so I couldn't make out who the people were, or if they were really alive or dead. But by the way they were moving, a kind of mindless shuffling, I knew that these were some of the dead that had come back.

A cold chill danced over my spine. How could this be happening?

I tried the police station again on my cell. We had no home phone, as we all had cell phones and had no need for it. Nobody was answering at the police station. No answer from Kelly or Derek.

I tried 911. The lines were completely jammed.

Not a big surprise.

I checked the laptop. The kid hadn't returned to his live streaming video. A view of an empty kitchen filled the screen.

There were a lot of other pleas for help on PheedMe.

News reports were not encouraging. The dead were growing quickly in numbers. A scratch or a bite would kill you within an hour. Soon after, you turn into one of them.

The military were out in tanks and humvees, but more and more of them were being taken down. The sheer numbers of the dead were making the task of killing them unmanageable. The rapidness with which a person turned was making it near impossible to keep their numbers down.

But more interesting were the reports and videos of the children and babies who had returned. It seemed that all of the kids who had vanished had reappeared over night.

All of them now had white blonde hair and strange, green eyes.

"Doe-doe!"

I jumped up and ran into the living room, where Jessie was standing on the couch looking out the window into the street. She pointed one small finger at the glass, touching it lightly. "Oook! Oook! A boy aside!"

As I approached the window, my breath caught in my throat. A boy of about nine years old with a shock of white hair stood under a street light, staring up at the window. He stared right at me as the dead wandered all around him.

And the strangest thing was that the dead didn't seem to bother with him at all.

MY INITIAL REACTION was that the kid gave me the

creeps. My second was that I needed to get him out of the street, before the dead realized that he was standing there and that he wasn't one of them.

He was still watching me. I waved him up. "Come on, kid. Slowly."

He just stood there, expressionless, watching me.

I was going to have to go out there and get him. "Damn it."

"Bad word, Doe-doe." Jessie wagged a finger at me.

"Sorry, Jess. Listen. Can you stay in here and be a good girl while Doe-Doe goes out and gets that little boy?"

Jessie nodded. "I a big girl."

"Yes, you are." Watching the kid for a long minute, I hoped I wasn't being an idiot going out there. If something happened to me trying to get that kid to safety, Jessie would be on her own.

But I couldn't leave him out there like that. The dead could turn their attention to him at any moment. I frowned. Why didn't he come up? Why did he just stand there like that?

He must be in shock. Must've lost his parents. Siblings, too maybe.

"Poor kid." I bit my lip, heart pounding, trying to ready myself for going out there.

"Yeah. Poe kid." Jessie's voice was full of sympathy. "Where his mommy? With my mommy?"

"I don't know, sweetie. I'll just be a minute. Stay here, okay?"

She nodded her head, and then turned back to the window.

I made my legs move and headed toward the door, listening for any movement outside. I heard nothing.

Slowly, I turned the knob and pulled the door open about an inch.

The smell hit me at the same time as the cold did. A strange, sulfuric smell, with the reek of rot beneath it.

If I breathed through my mouth, whatever was in the air would be on my tongue. I kept my mouth closed and dealt with the stench.

I peeked through the small opening I'd made. No one was out there.

Carefully, I closed the door behind me and walked quietly across the wooden porch and down the steps.

Nothing paid attention to me, yet. Just the little boy.

Again, I tried to wave him up. He remained still, gazing at me with those weird, expressionless eyes. With his coloring, I knew he had been one of the vanished. He had probably just come back from where he'd been, like Jessie had.

A dead woman shuffled past him, and now she was close enough for me to see that she'd been the woman who lived next door. She'd had a son.

Realization slammed into me. This had been the dark-haired kid who lived next door with her. She was a single mother. It had been just the two of them. But they'd been gone, visiting her parents in another state --- Connecticut --- maybe Vermont. I couldn't remember.

They were back, now.

She continued past him, moving slowly under the street light, and I could see that her eyes were milky white, her skin shot through with dark veins. She made strange gurgling noises deep in her throat.

Fear clawed at my belly and my heart slammed in my chest as I watched her move past him, not even looking at him.

He had to be in shock.

Was that why all these kids had white hair now? Shock? What had they seen while they were gone? Had it been that terrible?

I waited until she had walked several feet away, looked all around to make sure there weren't any dead near us, and moved as quickly and quietly as I could toward him.

"Hey, Danny. Are you okay?" I took his hand. It felt cold in mine.

He looked up at me, nodding slowly. His voice came out as a whisper. "Yes."

"Come on, buddy. Let's get you in the house. It's not safe out here." I gently tugged on his hand, starting to walk back toward the house, looking all around us. On the news I'd seen how fast these things could move when they had motivation to. Motivation being food --- the closest thing to eat being the living.

It seemed that the dead didn't like eating things that weren't moving and screaming while they tore into them, preferring instead the taste of hot blood, and the feeling of it spraying their faces.

My breaths came out in little pants, and my body broke out in a cold sweat. Just a few more feet and we'd be at the stairs to the porch.

A knock sounded above and I looked up, startled. Jessie was knocking on the window, giggling and yelling. She was thrilled that Danny was coming with me.

I turned and looked toward the street. Several of the dead were now walking toward the house, inhuman moans and grunts coming from their dead throats.

Hot fear shot through my chest. My mouth went dry. "Come on, Danny. Better move a little faster."

Then his hand was gone from mine and he was like a blur, moving toward the door.

I'd never seen a person move so fast.

He looked at me, and a slow smirk lifted the corners of his lips.

THIS DEFINITELY WASN'T LIKE the polite kid who lived next door and sometimes came over to the porch when Jessie and I came out here to play. These kids were different. I hadn't had a chance to look up what people were posting about their kids. But I sure as hell would now, the minute I got Danny settled in.

The kid gave me the creeps, but I couldn't just leave him outside. He was still a kid. Wasn't he?

I opened the door for him, and the second he walked in the apartment, Jessie was laughing and clapping. Her personality hadn't changed. She was still the bright and cheerful little girl she'd been before she'd vanished. Thank God.

"Danny! Yo hair aw white!" Jessie apparently didn't know that her hair had changed color, too.

But now looking at it, I realized that the eyebrows and eyelashes of both kids were also white. It wasn't so much that their hair had changed color as that the color had leached out of it.

Spooky.

"Have a seat, Danny. Would you like something to drink? A juice box? Milk? Water?"

Danny sat on the couch next to Jessica, who ran her fingers through his white hair.

"Nana, Danny?" Jessie asked him.

He looked up at her and said nothing, but Jessie stopped moving, staring back into his eyes. In a moment, she nodded, then climbed off the couch and toddled off into the kitchen.

I frowned, following her. She opened the fridge and grabbed a juice box in one small hand, then closed the fridge and toddled past me, back into the living room, and handed the juice box to Danny.

Again, he looked into her eyes.

Jessie smiled. "Yo welcome, Danny."

Danny hadn't said a word to her.

"How did you know what Danny wanted, Jessie? Did you guess?" I asked, already dreading her answer, because I knew what it would be.

"I just knowed." Jessie resumed playing with Danny's hair as he watched me silently with those eerie, pale eyes.

THE CREEPY KID wasn't talking. Not so that I could hear him, anyway. I found some cookies in the cupboard and put a bunch on a plate, putting it on the coffee table for him and Jessie.

Jessie beamed. "Choca ship!"

Danny looked down at the plate, then back at me.

I backed into the kitchen. Whatever his dealio was, he seemed to really like Jessie, and even be protective of her. But he looked at me like he didn't trust me.

Given current events, and God knew what else had happened to him, I didn't really blame him.

No. He's looking at you like he knows something you don't.

Just hang in there. Check the news. See what's up. You can figure out what to do with him later.

I tried my cell and got a message that the provider was

experiencing technical difficulties. Wonderful. So even if I got a phone number from Danny for his grandparents in Connecticut or Vermont, or wherever it was he and his mother had been, I couldn't call them.

I googled 'vanished kids return' and got a ton of hits; blog entries, videos, and people posing questions on forums.

All saying the same thing.

My kid is back but is different.

I viewed several videos of people recording their returned kids with their blank expressions and their eerie smiles. Kids seeming to talk to each other without moving their lips. Siblings having entire conversations without opening their mouths.

Parents were scared.

I saw more videos of white haired children walking the streets, some alone, and some in groups, amongst the dead.

The kids acted like the dead weren't even there, and the dead did the same with them.

But the most frightening thing I saw were videos, more and more of them, of children watching, completely emotionless, as the dead tore the living apart before their eyes.

With my hands pasted over my mouth, I watched in utter horror as a group of four siblings watched their parents, who were rushing them to the family car in their driveway, overcome by a large herd of the dead, tearing chunks from their flesh, taking them down as they shrieked in terror and agony.

The kids simply stood and watched, completely unaffected.

The person filming was a neighbor across the street, who kept saying, "Oh, my God. Oh, God. What the hell is wrong with these kids?"

I heard a gasp as one at a time, each of the four children lifted their shocking white heads, looked straight into the camera, and gave the same, creepy smirk.

As if they'd heard him.

"Jesus Christ almighty," the man recording said. "Save us all."

WHERE THE HELL were Derek and Kelly?

Deep down, I knew that something had happened to them. Rayback had said that he'd come back and check on me and see if Jessie had been brought back, by some miracle, sometime today. Unless I'd slept through his knocking earlier, he hadn't come. Neither had Derek and Kelly.

They aren't coming. You're on your own.

I sat in a big, fluffy chair in the corner of the living room while Jessie slept curled up to Danny on the couch. Danny lay behind her, one arm around her, eyes closed.

Do they still dream? How else had these kids changed? Would they ever be normal again? As normal as they could ever be after what had happened to them? Whatever that had been.

Happy that his spooky eyes weren't on me, I closed my own eyes and began to drift. The chaos and constant fear and worry had left me jittery and so tired. I was trying to find an answer, thinking of what to do. Ask Danny where his other family lived, like grandparents, aunts, uncles. I didn't want to be responsible for him.

Even though he was clearly great with Jessica, the kid scared me.

I opened my eyes and my heart froze in my chest.

He was looking right at me.

He knows what I'm thinking. Might as well say it out loud. "Danny, do you have any family we can take you to?"

Danny shook his head.

"What about the people you just visited with your mom? Your grandparents? Anyone?" I hated to bring her up, because she was one of the wandering now, but I had to know.

"They are all dead." His whisper sounded like dead leaves moving in the wind.

"How do you know that? There may be some who are alive. Maybe hiding out somewhere."

"No. They are dead. I know."

I stood up, looked out the window. The dead were still wandering the street. There were more of them. Each time I looked out the window, there were more of them.

Now groups of them were surrounding houses, trying to get in. Some doors hung open, and the dead shambled in and out.

They surrounded houses with closed doors, banging against them. They broke windows, climbing over each other to get inside.

Several of the dead were standing in the yard, looking up at the house.

"Oh, shit," I breathed, fear and panic twisting my gut and racing up my spine. I shot a look to Jessie. What about when the dead decided to try to get in?

"Don't worry," Danny said. "They won't come in here."

"They're looking right at the house, Danny." How long before they made their way up the stairs to the porch?

"They smell you inside," Danny said. "But they won't come in here with me and Jessie here."

I didn't ask why that should be true. Something told me

that hearing the answer would be more than my already panicked mind could bear.

I trusted that what he said was true.

But we couldn't stay in here forever.

"You are running out of time." His whisper was a strange crackle, like it was coming from a deep well.

I don't know what he is, but he isn't just a kid. Not anymore. I looked back at Danny. "What do you mean, Danny?"

He watched me with that blank look on his face and those weird green eyes. "This world is not yours anymore. There is nowhere for you to go."

"What are you talking about? Where did you kids go when you vanished? Do you remember?"

"It's like a dream. Of lights. Of knowing. We aren't the same. We're more, now."

"More what?" I said, fear and frustration raising the pitch of my voice.

He said nothing else. The corners of his lips lifted in that strange, knowing grin.

I WOKE UP, startled, my heart beating wildly against my chest. It froze when I looked over at the couch and saw that it was empty, except for a few tufts of hair lying where Jessie and Danny's head had been resting. It was dark, but the lamp over the couch was on. When I glanced toward the window, I saw my own image against the blackness beyond it.

It startled me. My eyes were large and wild looking. My skin was as pale as the dead outside. My hair, normally strategically messy because it's cut that way, now made me look like I'd been living on the streets for a while.

"Jessie?" Faintly, I heard her voice coming from down the hall. It echoed in the bathroom, but sounded odd. It was like she was talking from the other end of a long tunnel. "Jess?"

Something small and white lay on the couch cushion. I leaned in, looking more closely. A tooth; one of her little teeth.

White blonde hair lay scattered on the carpet, little white teeth dotting the spaces beneath and between the baby fine strands, leading from the couch to the hallway, stopping at the closed bathroom door.

I reached out and turned the knob. Locked.

A jolt of panic shot through me. "Jessica!"

"*Zoooooeeee.*" My name was drawn out on a low whisper that sounded like a hiss.

"Where is Jessica?" I pounded on the door. "Open the door."

"*Jeeeeessssicaaa is nooooooot heeeerreee.*" The sound of light splashing.

The hair lifted at the back of my neck and fear twisted in my stomach. "Where is she? Open the door!"

"*Goooo. Leeeave. Yoooou aaare ooout ooooof tiiiime.*"

The sound of a low giggle over the voice. Hisses overlapping each other. There was more than one in there. *One what?*

Splash Splash.

"I swear to God I will kick this door down!" I screamed.

I took a couple of steps back and prepared to make good on my promise.

The lock clicked and the door opened a couple of inches.

With my pulse beating in my neck and blood roaring in my ears, I stepped toward the door. Every cell of my being wanted to run. There was something behind the door that sent fear so raw and complete through me that every instinct told me to get out. Run out of the house and keep going.

But I wouldn't go without Jessica.

Please let her be okay. Please . . . he didn't hurt her. I pushed the door open.

Jessica was lying at the bottom of the tub, her eyes wide open, watching me. Her blonde hair floated all around her head, no longer attached to her scalp. Blood swirled upward from her mouth. She was at least a foot longer. As if she'd grown rapidly overnight. She gave me a gummy smile.

I stopped, terror paralyzing me to the spot. I couldn't tell if she was alive or dead. "Jessica!"

Danny knelt in front of her, trailing a hand in the water above her belly. He was bigger too, as if he'd grown a few years in a night. His hair was all gone. Locks of it lay all over the bathroom floor. I ran to the tub and grabbed her under the arms, lifting her up. Her head broke the surface of the water, and her hair stayed in the tub.

She sat up, smiling, and her teeth were missing.

"Oh, my God. Danny, what did you do to her?" I lifted her out of the water. She had to be twenty pounds heavier. I grabbed a towel and wrapped it around her, clutching her and walking backward out of the bathroom.

"*I aaaaam waaaatching heeeeer traaansfoooorm.*"

I ran down the hall, into Jessie's bedroom and locked the door, then laid her gently on my bed. My voice was high with fear and my entire body trembled as I worked to dry her off. "I'm going to get you to the hospital, Jessie. You're going to be fine. We need to get you dressed."

Jessie gave me a slow smile. "*It iiiiis oooooooookay, Zooooeeee. Iiiit dooooooes nooooot huuuurt.*"

"Jessie, what happened to your teeth?"

Then I heard her voice in my head as I worked to get her dressed. *They fell out, Zoe. I'm growing new ones. Look. Aren't they pretty?* She smiled widely, tilting her head back to show me.

And there they were. Several rows of tiny, razor sharp teeth poking through her gums.

YOU NEED TO GO NOW, Zoe. They are coming. The Jessica-thing's bizarre eyes tracked me as I backed away from her.

This wasn't Jessica. Not anymore. She was gone; turned into something alien. If some part of her was still in there, it wouldn't be for long.

"Who is coming?" I didn't want to look at her, but I couldn't look away. I watched in horror as she changed, and the abject terror I felt was complete. The world outside was going to shit. The person I cared about most in the world was gone --- or mostly gone. The last remnants of the love she felt for me warned me before being completely taken over.

The rest of them. The rest of us. They can't harvest you, Zoe. You are defective.

"I'm defective." My voice sounded far away and tinny as I tried to make sense of what the Jessica thing was telling me but it wasn't making sense. I had backed into her bedroom. I watched the doorway as the hissing down the hall grew louder.

She slid of the bed, and she pulled herself along the carpet toward me, her movements lizard-like.

Go now. They are almost here.

I ran to the door, slamming and locking it, then turned, my back pressed to the cold wood, looking in disbelief at what she was becoming.

She cocked her head at me, studying me as if I were some interesting species. To the new Jessica, maybe I was. Her movements had become snake-like. Her arms, torso and legs moved in a strange, serpent-like paddling manner. Her skull was growing, transforming; the forehead stretched backward, the back of her head lengthening into a dome-like shape. Her teeth slid through her gums, long and serrated.

I heard the sound of the front door opening, and hisses overlapping one another.

I headed toward her window, unlocked it and lifted it. It was second story. The drop wouldn't kill me. But the ever-growing group of zombies below the window would.

Thrown to the dead. Her head weaved side to side, like a cobra, and she sniffed the air, what used to be her nostrils in a now sunken nose flaring. *Or eaten. I can smell your blood, Zoe.*

I looked at her one last time; the strange, alien thing that used to be my niece. "The meteors. This is an invasion."

Her eyes, now completely serpent green, slid to the door, where the handle started turning.

I didn't wait to see what was on the other side of the door.

THANK God for all that tree climbing when I was a kid.

There was a huge old spruce tree with enormous branches stretching out toward the windows, and in all other directions. The branches closest to the window weren't strong enough to hold me, but further in, they grew thick. I needed to get onto the roof so that I could get a running start.

As I climbed out of the window, I grasped on to the gutter first, pulling myself up enough that I could swing a leg onto the edge of the roof. The snow that lay on top of the shingles had hardened. The temperature had dropped overnight, and although I was freezing, the hardened snow made it easier for me to gain purchase and pull myself up onto the roof. I said a silent prayer of thanks that I hadn't taken my boots off after going out to get Danny. I didn't have a jacket on, but the thick hoodie I wore over my old sweatshirt kept the worst of the chill from my skin --- for the moment.

That and the fear and adrenalin spiking through my body kept me warm, but I'd have to find a jacket to wear soon or I'd freeze to death.

I wasn't going back into the house to get mine.

Scrambling up onto the roof, I crab walked backwards, working my way up. If I wasn't careful I'd slide down into the waiting claws of the dead, who would happily break my fall.

Even with the moans and strange animal shrieks they made, I heard the hissing sound coming from beneath the roof line, where I'd just climbed out of Jessica's window. I sat, frozen, watching for her --- for it, my breaths coming in little pants.

The ovaloid head rose up and weaved, snake-like, upward, emerging from above the roof line. The thing that used to be Jessica spotted me, and a long, black tongue slipped out from between the serrated teeth and licked its lips.

I scrambled backward, moving higher up onto the roof, my mind racing. I was trapped. The dead were waiting below, and this reptilian Jessica- thing was slithering toward me. It moved on its belly, zigzagging upward, the insectile legs paddling upward.

The knife was still in my boot, sitting in the sheath I'd made for it from thick elastic and Velcro. I'd thought, at the time, that I'd never really have to use it. But I'd used it already in the last two days, and I was about to use it again. I reached down and wrapped my fingers around the Uberti, pulling it out of my boot and gripping it tightly. If I dropped it, it was over.

Tears blurred my vision as I watched the thing slide upward toward me. Was there anything of my niece left in this horrific thing? My voice cracked when I spoke. "Jessica."

"*Zooooooeeee.*" The thing hissed in reply. The tongue slipped out again, snapping in the air. "*I'm soooooo huuuungry.*"

My entire body trembled as I clutched the knife tightly in my shaking hand.

"*Juuuuust a taaaaaste, Zoooooeeee.*" It seemed that soon the thing wouldn't be able to form words at all. The words were becoming less and less audible with every passing second.

The thing was only a few feet from me now. The eyes, greenish gold, sliding in sockets that had shrunken back, the lids no longer there. It snapped jagged, shark-like teeth as it approached.

There was nowhere for me to go. This thing would

follow me. Silent sobs shook me as I waited. I knew I'd only get one chance.

Scaled legs scuttled upward, and the body zig-zagged as it reached my feet. I waited for it to move a little further up, praying that it wouldn't take a bite out of one of my legs before I had the chance to stab it.

Moving forward with quick side to side movements, the elongated neck stretched toward my face. It was so close now. Drool slid over its teeth and down the greenish chin, dripping into the snow on both sides of me. The snow sizzled, holes steaming where the thing's saliva hit it.

A couple of drops hit my hoodie, burning holes into it. My belly stung where its spit made its way onto my skin.

I screamed, it felt like I was being burned by cigarettes.

She was standing right over me. In a second, she would kill me if I missed.

What used to be lips stretched over the teeth as the mouth opened, head titled back. Eyes rolled back into the tipped head and a long, throaty screech came from the depths of her throat.

I flipped the knife over handed and drew my hand back.

When her head came whipping down toward my face, I brought my arm down with every ounce of strength I had, aiming for the left eye.

The knife sank into the strange, green-gold orb to the hilt, and the creature shrieked, a sound of utter surprise, rage and agony.

I yanked the Uberti out and jammed it into the throat, slicing sideways.

Black blood spurted, spraying onto the snow.

She gurgled, her eyes rolling in her ovoid head.

I hauled back my leg and kicked the thing in the chest,

sending it sliding down the roof, legs skittering for purchase. She slid over the edge of the roof and vanished.

Before I could catch my breath, another one started to emerge, the elongated head rising above the roof line, golden orbs that used to be human, child eyes scanning the roof top.

If I let it get up here, I'd have to fight this one, too. I scrambled down toward it as it rose upward, two lizard-like arms pulling itself upward.

As I reached it, its mouth opened and it snapped its teeth at me, its black tongue slipping out and moving across its teeth. It began moving onto the roof toward me.

Placing one boot on its chest, I plunged the blade of my Uberti into the left orb-like eye to the hilt. As it screamed, I wrenched the knife out and jammed it into the right.

The shriek was unearthly.

I tugged the blade out and put the handle between my teeth, biting down on it. I needed my hands free.

I took a few steps back, then ran and leapt into the spruce tree.

The branches shook and snow flew up at me from crackling twigs, but I'd landed deeply enough into the tree that they held me. If I'd weighed ten pounds more, they might not have. I thanked my lucky stars that I was built like a stick. All the times I cursed having to shop in the junior girls section for clothes; all the years I wished I was curvier, sexier looking.

I'd finally found a reason to like my slight frame. Go figure.

Spruce needles poked into the skin of my hands, my face, scratching me, but I barely noticed. I could hear the dead below me, groaning, grunting, and beneath those sounds, the hisses. The hisses were growing louder, overlapping --- more and more of them.

I straddled the thickest part of the branch closest to the trunk of the spruce. Shivering, I peered through the snow speckled needles at the house and the ground below.

The two reptilian things were lying on the ground, black blood spreading around them. The dead wandered away from them, keeping their distance. If it weren't for those reptilian things, I'd be petrified of the dead. It was a horror movie come to life.

But these snake, lizard things made the dead look like small potatoes in comparison.

Clinging to the branches, quivering in fear and cold, I wondered why I was fighting so hard to survive in this new, dead world --- this invasion.

Was this what I had to live for? Running, hiding, and fighting?

It was probably easier just to opt out and die. Leave the horror of it all. I had no one left. I knew it deep in my bones.

As I watched more of the lizards, which is what I'd decided to call them, climb out of the window and skitter up onto the roof, searching for me, I knew that I really had no one left in the world. They'd been eaten by the dead, or by the lizards.

I was completely, utterly alone.

THREE

I watched and waited. Now so cold, I was afraid I'd fall. My hands were so numb I could barely feel them. If I didn't get out of this tree, I'd freeze to death or I'd fall to the dead becoming a nice human Popsicle for them to dig into.

Or worse, the reptiles would find me.

They had left the roof. I'd counted fifteen of them. They'd swarmed the house, looking for humans. But I was already gone.

They'd moved out into the streets, slithering and skittering into the other houses.

Screams and shrieks cut through the frozen air.

I wanted to cry, but swallowed it down. I couldn't afford for ice to form on my face. Instead, I hugged the branches with numbing arms, waiting.

It was the darkest part of the night, just before dawn, and I could see silhouettes of the lizards as they dragged people out, pulling them into the woods that lined the backs of the houses. There were fields beyond the woods, and the reptiles disappeared into the snow, dragging screaming people behind them.

Squeezing my eyes shut, I held on to the branch, trembling, trying to shut out the screams and the dragging sounds.

Underground. They were taking them underground. Why? To eat?

Oh, my God. Oh, God.

I remembered something Jessie had said to me, one day in the summer as we played ball in the back yard, not far from where I hid in the branches, shivering. She'd stopped playing, dropping the ball and laying on the ground, her ear pressed to the grass.

"What are you doing, Jess?" I smiled.

"Heah dem?" She'd whispered.

"Hear who, sweety?" I laid down next to her and pressed my ear to the grass. I didn't hear anything, except the noise of the street: birds, cars, people talking.

"Someone down dere." Her face was full of concentration.

I thought she was playing a game. Or that her imagination had run wild. Or that she was hearing a mole moving around in the ground. Lord knew there were holes everywhere in that back yard. All kinds of animals made the ground their home: moles, groundhogs, squirrels, chipmunks. But it wasn't animals that she had been hearing that day. She'd been hearing the reptiles, preparing their takeover.

So if I got brave enough to climb down from the tree and jump the ten feet or so down from the lowest branch, chances were that they'd come running.

Or slithering. Like reptiles do.

That was if the dead didn't get to me first.

You are screwed.

No. No you are not. You didn't survive an almost gang

rape to die like that. Hells, no. So get a grip. You are not giving up.

I wouldn't have a choice if I didn't figure out a way to get out of the tree and into one of the houses, and get warm.

The screams had stopped. Except for the grunts and moans of the dead, there was no sound. I opened my eyes and squinted as I gazed around at the houses and the yards. The doors of every house within my sights had been left open by the lizards. In the gauzy light of dawn, I could see the dead shuffling around in yards, on porches, and through the windows of the houses. They were like scavengers, looking around to see if anything had been left.

The clean-up crew.

Get moving.

There was a tall wooden fence between this yard and the next door neighbor's. I climbed down onto the lower branches of the spruce, then shimmied across, as close to the thinning end as I dared, feeling it bend with my weight. I used gravity to allow the branch to lower me down toward the fence.

My fingers were so cold I wondered if I might lose some or all of them. I used my arms as much as I could, because my fingers were so numb.

My boots found the fence, and I carefully climbed down onto it, using my arms, hooking them around the wooden boards. Thankfully, they weren't picketed --- just boards cut straight across. That meant I wouldn't impale myself as a result of my numb and almost useless hands. It was amazing how happy, in a life and death crisis, a person could be for small things that helped him or her to survive.

Carefully hooking my arms over the wood, I climbed over the fence and let myself hang for a moment, preparing my feet for the shock of dropping down if I slipped. Then

I'd use the toes of my boots to slide down as best I could, making as minimal an impact on the ground as possible.

The snow would help cushion the impact, but I didn't know how good the reptiles' hearing was. Or maybe they sensed vibrations. Fear paralyzed me for a long moment, and I hung, the toes of my boots resting on a cross board about two feet from the bottom of the fence.

Keep moving. You're almost there.

There was no helping the muted *thud* my boots caused on the crunchy snow as I landed. I hoped the shuffling of the dead helped obscure the sound. It was a small stroke of luck that the fence surrounding the back yard of this house was built to keep their dog in the yard, and it also kept the dead out. The dog, a Boxer crossed with some other mastiff type dog, trotted nervously around the yard. When it spotted me, its' ears lifted and a quizzical look came across its face. There was a jagged cut across its back, glistening with fresh blood. A war wound from trying to defend his people, no doubt.

He stood watching me, body and head alert, but seemed to know that I wasn't a threat.

Maybe it had been all the Cheetos I'd tossed over the fence for him when Jessie and I had been out here playing.

Moving as lightly on my feet as I could, I winced as the snow broke and crunched beneath my boots. The dog ran over to me, tail wagging, clearly happy that I was no longer alone. I shared the feeling.

"Come on, boy." With trembling, numb hands, I patted him on his blocky head and he followed me to the house. The sliding glass door left open by the reptiles after dragging Mr. and Mrs. Doriga away, kicking and screaming across the snow and into the trees.

They had a teenage daughter, Luka, who was just

fifteen years old. I shuddered as I thought of what had happened to her. I didn't remember seeing her being dragged away. But that didn't mean that she was safe. I'd been busy fighting for my life while others on the street had lost theirs.

Keep moving.

I left the sliding door open, in case I had to get out fast. If the house was empty, I'd come back and close it. The back yard was clear of the dead, so it was safe for the moment.

Right now I needed shelter; a place to think for a little while. I had to assess the situation, map out a plan, and figure out how to get through this.

The dog stayed close at my heels, and followed me up the stairs. There was a closed door at the top. I pressed my ear to the cool wood, listening for any movement.

The dog lifted his ears, doing the same.

"Do you hear anything?" I asked him. I figured if he did hear something, he'd be a good warning indicator.

He stared at the door, ears twitching, but didn't make any signal that there was anyone in the house.

This dog wasn't a barker. The only time I'd heard him bark was when his people had been dragged away. I'd squeezed my eyes shut at the time, trying to block out their screams.

The dog wouldn't draw the attention of the dead, or the lizards.

Slowly, I turned the knob. "Stay close, buddy."

I stepped into a kitchen, standing still, looking around and listening. There was a door off the kitchen left open, and freezing air swirled around the kitchen, lifting the edges of photos and post-it notes on the fridge door. Why were there no dead in here? Or had they moved to another room in the house?

Slowly, I moved to the door, peeking around it to the stairs and yard outside.

I had my answer.

A wheelchair lay tipped over in the yard, and several of the dead were busy tearing into the old man who had been apparently either trying to get away from the house or into it. There lay a walker a few feet away, and the old lady who had used it next to it. She was also being eaten.

The grandparents. I'd seen them making their slow way to and from the Dorigas' Honda Pilot before.

The dead were busy now, but they wouldn't be forever.

I quietly pulled the door shut and locked it.

There was no movement. I knew there had to be an open door somewhere, where the dead had come in.

Moving carefully I started checking the rest of the house. I went room by room, looking for any dead that might've made their way in. They were quiet, which made them lethal if you weren't careful. They may not be fast, but they were stealthy.

The dog stayed right beside me, and I was thankful for his company. I didn't feel so alone, now. He didn't seem to want to move far without me, either. I couldn't blame him.

When we'd checked the entire house for the dead and found it clear, I let out a deep breath.

"I think we're safe for now, bud." I patted the dog's head. My horror-addled mind tried to remember his name but came up with nothing.

Kneeling down, I rubbed my hands over his head, then looked at the tags on his collar.

The name on the tag was Hank. "Hank," I said. His ears lifted and his tail thudded against the floor. Then I remembered Mrs. Doriga calling for him. I'd thought she was calling Tank. That name would've suited him fine, as big as he was.

"Pleased to meet you." I kept my voice low. "We're in trouble here. I guess you already know that."

Hank licked my face. The gash on his back looked ugly, but I didn't think it was too bad.

I found the bathroom down a hallway off the living room. There was some antiseptic spray and some antibiotic ointment in the cabinet. Hank was close on my heels. I bent down, sprayed the antiseptic onto his long gash. The spray was supposed to be numbing, so I hoped it helped his pain. I then squeezed ointment all along the wound.

He whimpered lightly, but didn't move.

I patted him on the head. "Good boy. You're so brave."

Taking the medicine with me, I looked around the house. In the teenager's room, I found a canvas backpack. I dumped it onto her bed and stuffed the medicine into it.

I looked through her clothes and found a pair of yoga pants that would fit me. In her closet I found a ski jacket and black windbreaker pants. They had an elastic waist, so they fit me okay, if a little big. The girl was a skier. Lucky for me.

Scanning the room, my gaze stopped on a cork board covered in pictures. The girl, small and blonde, smiled into the camera in every photo. I'd seen her coming and going, but had never spoken to her. There were many selfies with friends. She seemed like a popular, happy girl. A birthday card hung on a push pin. I lifted a corner with a finger and read the short blurb handwritten in loopy script.

To my best friend in the world. Hope your year is full of love, friends, and laughter.

Lots of love, Taylor.

I wondered if Taylor had escaped the reptiles and the dead.

Maybe Luka had, too.

I blinked back tears and swallowed down a lump in my throat.

It was time to pack up. This house wouldn't be safe for long.

I packed the backpack with the bare minimum of what I'd need if I had to take off fast.

Back in the bathroom I threw ibuprofen and bandages into the back pack.

In the kitchen I found Hank's food and filled two freezer bags full. Again, he looked at me quizzically.

"Well, you're coming with me, aren't you?"

His tail wagged at the tone of my voice. He understood that we'd be going somewhere, and he was apparently all for not being left alone to starve.

"Are you hungry?"

His tail thumped the floor and he stood up. He walked toward the kitchen, throwing me a look that said, "Well? What are you waiting for?"

My entire body ached as I stood, and I looked through the slats in the vertical blinds before heading into the kitchen. The backyard was quiet, and flooded with bright sunshine. The snow glinted in the light, looking like diamond chips.

The fence was too tall for me to see into our back yard, but I knew the dead were walking around out there. The lizards seemed to be gone for now. But there was no way to be sure.

Hank came up beside me and placed his head beneath my hand. "I'm sorry, buddy. Just assessing the situation out there. Looks quiet for now."

We went into the kitchen and I poured Hank a full bowl of food. His water bowl was being fed by a gallon bottle turned upside down into his dish, so that would be fine for a while. While Hank ate, I lifted a corner of the curtain covering the window in the kitchen door. I peeked outside. There were several dead still eating the old lady and old man, but many of them had left the streets to search in the houses.

There were no lizards moving around the streets.

"I think the lizards are nocturnal, Hank." I kept my voice low, not wanting to draw the attention of the dead in the front yard.

Hank lifted his head and looked at me, still chewing his kibble.

"I don't think they like the daylight."

He walked over and sat next to me. I sat on the kitchen floor, leaning my back against the cupboards, and he lay down next to me.

"But they may be back tonight, to do another sweep. See what they can find." My chest tightened at the thought, and my breath quickened. If I wasn't careful, I'd go into a full panic. It would be easy to just lose it. Scream hysterically. I felt like my sanity was slipping. Was I the only person left in the world? Had everyone been eaten? Or were there others, hiding away, like me?

"If we're careful, we can move around in the day time. But you need to stay right with me, Hank. It's way too dangerous to go around joy sniffing. You know?"

Hank did know. I could feel it in the bunched muscles beneath his fur. In the way he pushed right up against me.

"We'll be okay if we're careful. We won't let them get us."

We sat on the cold linoleum and I began to try to form some kind of plan to keep us alive.

WE SAT like that for a long time. The cold and the shock of what was happening had settled deep into my muscles and bones. I felt sluggish and so tired. Like I could sleep for an entire year.

But I knew that if I didn't get moving, Hank and I would both end up dead, one way or the other. The lizards apparently weren't interested in Hank, but the dead would be. They didn't seem to be really picky about what they ate.

My stomach felt hungry and queasy at the same time, and I felt weak. Being outside in the cold, hanging onto a tree branch for hours had given me a case of the shivers that wouldn't go away.

Looking up at the cupboards, I tried to get up the gumption to push myself up. Maybe if I ate something, I'd start to feel warm again.

I scanned cupboards and found some peanut butter and a lot of other things to eat. Crackers, cookies, dried fruit, and granola bars. There were cans of soup and stew. In the fridge I found bread and an assortment of lunch meats, cheeses and vegetables. I slapped a peanut butter sandwich together and began choking it down. Before leaving, I'd make another sandwich and maybe put some string cheese, granola bars and dried fruit into a freezer bag in case we didn't make it back here. I found some bottled water and put a few bottles into my backpack. Some dog biscuits went in there, too.

Not knowing what the world beyond this street was like terrified me. I forced myself to breathe, because I kept catching myself holding my breath. The fear of the reptiles coming back for me or the dead finding a way in tightened my throat to the point that I had to keep swallowing.

Breathe. One step at a time. You're safe for the moment. What's next?

Once I knew what I was dealing with, I'd be able to formulate more of a plan. Right now, the only plan I had was to go out and assess the situation, and try to find others who had survived the first night of the invasion.

I finished my sandwich and drank down most of a bottle of water, then I looked at the huge clock on the wall above the stove. It read 11:31. It was December, so it would be dark by 4:30.

Until then, I hoped the only threat Hank and I had to worry about were the dead.

Come sundown, we needed to find a safe hideout.

IN LUKA'S closet I found a pair of UGG boots that looked warm. They were size seven. My size. I found some warm winter socks in one of her drawers and gladly exchanged my hole covered ones for those. The UGGs hugged my feet and warmed them instantly.

I risked waiting another half hour until the last two deadies had wandered off in search of something more to eat. The bones of the old lady and old man had been picked pretty clean. I wondered, as I screwed up my courage to open the kitchen door, if the dead walking had been incidental in the invasion or if they really were the cleaning crew. The seemed to be taking care of the leftovers that the lizards had no use for, or hadn't gotten at yet.

Judging by the way what used to be Jessica had reacted to the smell of my blood, I figured I fell into the latter group.

Hank was a leftover.

I was determined that we'd live another day. One day at a time, my mother had said when she was back on the wagon.

Only for us, I thought it was more like one minute at a time. If we lasted another day, I'd consider it a real achievement.

Maybe we could eventually be in the survival of the dead and alien invasion Olympics.

I snorted. The punchiness was getting to me. But then, maybe that was what would keep me going.

The remains of Mr. and Mrs. Doriga were scattered across the side yard. The dead, or the lizards, had made a meal of them. The Dorigas hadn't been taken by the lizards, so they must have been too old for their liking.

Except maybe for a meal. It was hard to tell who had torn into them, the lizards or the dead. Maybe both had. I averted my eyes and let out a shaky breath. I had to keep it together.

Hank looked up at me and lifted his ears. I patted his head and kept walking across the lawn. There was no car in the driveway. "We need a car, Hank."

Hank took off and ran toward the garage. Apparently he was used to car rides. The garage door was open, and the current model white Honda Pilot sat inside, looking pristine, like it had been recently washed.

Grandma and Grandpa had been coming for a Christmas visit, so it likely had been.

Suddenly Hank's hackles went up and a low growl came from deep inside of his throat.

There was something in that garage.

Gripping my knife, I slowly approached the garage, wincing at the crunching snow beneath my boots.

Two of the dead were trudging around the car. A little girl with no hair turned slowly to look at me. She was thin and hallow looking, and the circles under her eyes were deep and purple. She wore a pair of pink flannel pajamas with stars and moons all over them. She wore a white sock with purple frills on one foot. The other was bare.

I'd heard of this little girl. Sidney Curtis. There had been a collection for her about a month ago. She had a brain tumor, and friends of the family had been raising money for her medical bills. Her family had mortgaged their house twice to pay for everything that she'd needed.

I recognized her mother from the pictures on the news and the website. I'd donated twenty-five dollars to her fund. The Sidney Fund.

Looking at Sidney now, I felt a mixture of horror and complete and utter sadness. I hoped that she'd died before the world had gone to hell.

Then, as she shambled toward me, growling deep in her dead throat, it occurred to me that she hadn't vanished. She hadn't been one of the abducted children.

Because she was sick.

Apparently the aliens didn't want, or couldn't use, terminally ill sick kids.

Hank growled back at her, backing down the drive way. He was the smart one of the two of us, because I headed toward her.

As she reached me, arms out, hands grasping, I jammed my knife through her eye. She went down soundlessly, weighing so little that it made almost no impact on the snow.

Her mother walked toward me, short, red hair sticking

up in all directions. She didn't weigh much either. But then, I didn't imagine she'd eaten much, with her nine year old daughter dying a little more each day before her eyes.

Her jeans and white sweater hung on her skinny frame, and the area where Sidney must've bitten her was dark red. The blood had spread and dried. Her throat was all but completely torn out. Huge, gaping wounds left her neck weak, and her head hung awkwardly to the side as she walked toward me, jaw hanging slack.

"I am so sorry," I murmured. Not for what I was about to do, but for what she'd been through before she'd ended up as a deadie. Watching her child suffer and fade each day. The pain she must've endured was unimaginable to me. It seemed the most cruel and atrocious thing to happen to her.

I wondered if there was anything left of the person she'd been, behind those dead eyes. But then, it didn't matter. Killing the thing she'd become would be the ending of all of her suffering.

Stepping forward, I jabbed my knife sideways, through her ear, and ripped it back out, watching her fall on top of her daughter.

Hank growled again, looking toward the street.

Turning, I noted that two more deadies had left the houses they'd been searching for fresh meat, and were heading our way. More would be joining them soon, I was sure.

"Let's go, Hank." I ran into the garage, hoping that the keys were left in the Pilot.

Nope.

I looked around the garage frantically. "Please, please don't let them be in the house."

Hank growled again, louder.

The two deadies were slowly but surely making their way up the driveway, and three more weren't far behind.

I looked around, panic spiking adrenalin through my veins. Mr. Doriga seemed to have spent a lot of time here. Every man needs a man cave. There was a long counter at the back of the garage, and cabinets above it.

Hank followed close behind as I began whipping open the cabinet doors.

The deadies groaned a mere few feet behind me.

One cabinet door left. I held my breath.

On the back of it hung several keys.

But only one that would belong to a Honda Pilot.

I grabbed the key, spinning around as Hank barked wildly. He'd backed up to the wall, refusing to leave me. I shoved the key into the pocket of my jacket and gripped the knife.

The closest deadie was almost close enough to kiss me. I recognized him as a hot guy that used to jog up the street every morning. He stood in front of me, shirtless. Still, strangely, looking hot even though he was dead and drooling at me. He still sported a rippling six pack, even if he did look slightly grayer.

"Too bad." Shaking my head in regret, I brought my knee back and booted him in the stomach, sending him stumbling backward, then plunged my knife through the eye of a middle aged man who'd lived down the street and had given me the willies, watching me with a dirty leer each time I walked past his house.

"I've wanted to do that for a long, long time, creeper." I pulled my knife out of his eye and shoved him backwards with my boot.

I risked a glance at the counter behind me and found a hammer. "Nice!"

Hank was being chased by a heavyset deadie who was doing her undead version of calling him, which was to toddle after him in a stumbling, drunk looking stagger and grunt.

"Hey!" I shouted.

She stopped and turned, then came toward me.

"That's right. Come on over here, Mable." I didn't know what her name was, but Mable seemed to suit her pretty well. Her mouth opened and closed as she walked toward me. Her hot pink glasses hung lopsided on her face, and the blood covering her chin, chest and hands suggested that she'd dined fairly recently.

I swung the hammer back, bringing the claw end of it down on her forehead. It gave a loud crunch breaking her skull. Grimacing, I yanked it out. She stood, confused, but didn't drop. I swung it down on her forehead again. Still, she stood, swaying.

More deadies were making their way across the street. Two more were shambling up the driveway.

"Third time's a charm." This time, I aimed for her eye. I swung the claw through the milky orb, and it sank in with a wet, slopping sound. Finally, she did drop.

If Hank and I didn't get out of there now, we'd be quickly over run. The dead didn't move quickly, and one, two or even three might not be too hard to kill, but in greater numbers they would be lethal.

I opened the driver's door to the Pilot and Hank didn't wait for the invite, hopping in and jumping into the back seat with a little whine.

The Pilot started up like a dream. It was brand spanking new.

"Never thought I'd be driving one of these any time soon," I said to Hank. "Nice ride."

It even drove over Mable without a problem.

"SO NOW WE have a hammer and a knife, but I think we should try to find at least one gun. What do you think, Hank?"

Hank was still lying in the back seat of the Pilot. He seemed content to occasionally look out the windows at the ever-deadening world.

And it *was* becoming a dead world. Things were so much worse on the main roads. Cars had run off the roads, or had crashed. The dead roamed the streets. I was witness to people being eaten alive, before my eyes.

One thing I hadn't thought of was how vicious the living could be to each other.

The dead and the aliens were a threat, but many of the living were just as frightening. I watched people being pulled from their cars and left for dead in the middle of the road by brutal carjackers and scavengers, who stole their vehicles and belongings.

I saw a mother and infant be swarmed by the dead.

My sense of humor left me.

I sobbed as I drove through the streets as quickly as I could without crashing or running over any of the living. Stopping would mean death for me and Hank. We'd be left for dead and likely wouldn't survive more than a few minutes, both of us torn apart as we screamed for help that wouldn't come.

Tears blurred my vision and I gasped for breath. I made it through one of the busiest streets and took a side road to avoid more swarms of scavengers and dead.

Hank and I were safe in the Pilot for the moment. The

Dorigas had just filled the tank, but eventually we'd have to stop for gas.

I drove the side streets, weaving my way out of the city as quickly and stealthily as I could manage in a blinding white Honda Pilot. The guns would have to wait. I was getting us the hell out of the city.

I took the first road out toward the most rural town in the area. I drove dirt roads for miles, heading past fairgrounds that hosted a country fair every summer. My favorite one, complete with horse pulls and country crafts.

Those days were over.

When I was sure that Hank and I were far enough in the middle of nowhere to stop for a pee break, I stopped the Pilot in the middle of the dirt road and let Hank out.

The wind had picked up, and the air felt raw on my face. Luka's ski jacket and my mother's hat helped to keep me warm, but the cold still found a way to chill be to me the core.

There were no sounds out here. It was deathly silent. The snow lifted in the wind and swirled in little tornados over the white blanketed fields. A crow flew down from a tree and hopped around on the road a few yards away from us. It cocked its head from side to side, black eyes studying me curiously. The thing gave me the willies. There were plenty of dead things for it to eat, just south of here.

Let's make this quick. I squatted on the side of the road and emptied my painfully full bladder, letting out a relieved sigh as Hank did his business a few feet away from me. He didn't waste any time getting back to the truck, pacing around in front of it like he was afraid someone or something was out there, and would get us.

Maybe he knew something I didn't.

As I pulled up my pants, it hit me all at once.

I'd been so distracted by the dead and the horror of how brutal the living could be to each other, that I'd forgotten about the threat just on the horizon, just a couple of hours away.

There were fields surrounding us, and beyond those were woods.

Just the kind of place the reptiles loved to make their new home.

And the sun was steadily sinking in the sky.

I DROVE A LITTLE FURTHER, looking for a place that Hank and I could hide out. Part of me regretted leaving the safety of the Doriga's house, but then, when darkness fell, it may not be safe at all. There weren't any houses out here, so the reptiles may not have burrowed down into the ground this far out of the city.

But then, they may have.

I really had no intention of finding out.

My mind raced. If we didn't find a place to hide out, we'd have to spend the night in the Pilot. It was cold, and running the truck for heat would burn out the gas pretty quick. We needed to find shelter.

The Pilot was quiet as it moved along the snow caked country road. I kept the speed down to thirty miles an hour, sweeping both sides of the field for houses. There had to be farms out here.

We passed a dilapidated, abandoned shack, the ceiling of which had caved mostly in. I ditched any idea of spending the night there. Having the shack fall in on us wouldn't help us. If we survived, being trapped under broken debris and waiting for something to eat us was not a happy thought.

After another few miles my search became more frantic. The light had become murky. Long shadows steadily stretched from the woods over the fields toward us. I'd never noticed how fast darkness gathered in the wintertime before.

Hank growled, then gave a low bark.

I looked at him in the rearview. He was watching an area beyond the left window.

Following his gaze, I saw what he was growling at and my blood froze in my veins.

There was movement, out near a copse of trees not far off the road.

Something was watching us.

FOUR

I hit the lock button and felt a small measure of comfort when all of the locks clicked, but that feeling didn't last long.

In the gloom I saw two reptilian shapes moving low to the ground, dome-like heads moving up and down as if sniffing the air. Either they smelled my piss or they smelled me. Maybe both.

I smell your blood, Jessica had said.

Before I could even turn the key, something thumped against the passenger window.

My heart leapt into my throat as I jumped, then instinctively ducked down, looking up for the source of the impact.

I saw long claws scratching at the glass as the thing climbed on top of the Pilot. I looked up. The moon roof was closed, the reptilian banging at it with the force of hunger behind it. Dents began forming in the panel.

Two other reptilians jumped at the truck. One climbed onto the hood of the car and stared in at me. Its mouth yawned opened in an unearthly howl and saliva dripped over the rows of jagged teeth. The eyes were a strange grey, and it snapped its teeth at the windshield, trying to bite through it.

I froze, paralyzed, as the thing knocked its head at the windshield.

When that didn't work, it brought one arm back, its scaled chest lifting with the effort, and smashed its arm down onto the glass.

Hank barked wildly, then jumped into the passenger seat and sniffed the keys hanging from the ignition.

It broke my paralysis and I turned the key. The Pilot obeyed, starting easily. But there were two reptiles on the roof and one on the hood, and I didn't think we'd make it far before one of them burst through. The moonroof was giving, and the two reptiles now peered in at me through the small opening, strange grey eyes looking right into mine. Then, sniffing at the ever widening crack.

I jammed my foot on the gas pedal, and the reptile on the hood was thrown off. It scrambled through the air, falling on its haunches. Jumping up, it ran at the Pilot and jumped easily back on, skittering up the hood, its claws making little scratching sounds as it climbed toward the windshield.

My mind was blank with terror as I kept my foot jammed down on the gas. Hank barked madly at the moon roof, standing on the passenger seat with his paws on the back of the seat. His scare tactics weren't working.

Neither was my crazy driving.

These things were not easy to shake.

"Hang on, Hank!" I slammed the brake, and all three reptiles slid off the truck.

Hank was thrown from the seat and banged into the back of mine.

I hit the gas and ran over the reptilian that had been on

the hood. One scaled arm thumped on the hood when I turned the wheel and the Pilot's tires rolled over it with a loud crunch.

I laughed madly, looking back at it in the rear view. "You made the ugliest hood ornament ever, asshole!"

The other two reptiles skittered over to it. Its head had been crushed under the truck wheels. They sniffed it, heads tilting this way and that, then came bounding after me.

I didn't think I'd be so lucky again, but I had no choice. There was no other way to kill them without getting myself and Hank killed.

Killing us both in a firey truck accident wasn't ideal, but preferable to the alternative.

I slowed, watching as the reptilians bounded up the back of the Pilot, shuddering as I got a close look at their undersides, which were covered in scales. I'd never been a fan of snakes, and these things were like living nightmares.

"Brace yourself, Hank." Hank sat on the floor, where he'd stayed since being thrown from the back seat.

Fear clutched my belly as I hit the gas.

The two reptiles slid backwards from the Pilot's roof and landed on the road behind me.

Quickly, I put the Pilot in reverse and stomped the gas, driving over both of them.

Their bones snapped and crunched beneath the tires.

It was music to my ears.

I drove further backward, then stopped and put the truck in drive.

Both reptiles were still alive, trying to crawl toward the Pilot; their crushed limbs moving uselessly.

I had to give them points for determination and effort.

Stomping the gas, the pilot gained momentum and drove over the remaining two.

I whooped like a lunatic, cackling as I raced down the road.

The pilot's wheels slid and the truck skidded sideways, and the last thing I was aware of before hitting my head on the steering wheel was spinning into the field toward the snowy woods which looked as pretty as a Christmas card.

I AWOKE to Hank licking my face and barking. When I opened my eyes, it was full dark outside, and I was looking at the sky, hanging upside down, caught by the seatbelt.

"Oh, shit." My head hurt, and blood had leaked into one of my eyes. I was able to move my arms, and wiped a hand over the eye. It came back slippery, and slightly congealed. It looked like the bleeding had stopped.

It was dark in the truck, and the engine was dead. Other than Hank's quiet whimpering, there was no sound.

My head throbbed fiercely, and I was sure that I had a fair sized goose egg at the very least, a concussion possibly. I didn't want to waste any more time assessing my injuries.

Hank seemed fine. He might be a little banged up, but he was hopping around the front of the car frantically.

His way of telling me to move my ass. We needed to get out of there.

"Are there any more of those things out there, Hank?" I whispered to him.

As if he understood me, he looked out the cracked windshield. He whimpered as he looked up at my window, which was now above us.

What the hell were we going to do? The truck was toast. How far would we get before more of those things came after us? It wasn't dawn yet, and they'd hear our footsteps in the snow.

"We need to wait until daylight, Hank."

He licked my face.

I found the button to disengage the seatbelt and it let go, dropping me downward.

The movement sent an unpleasant jab through my head.

How did those things not hear the car accident?

The simple answer was that they had. I didn't think I'd been out for more than a few minutes. They were likely right outside the window, investigating.

Barely whispering, I said, "Hank, be quiet. Don't bark. Shhhh."

He lay down next to me, watching me with scared eyes which flicked toward the window every second or so.

I closed my eyes and strained my ears to hear if there were any sounds near the car.

There. I heard a shifting, scuttling sound in the snow right outside, to the left of the truck.

Hank lifted his head.

"Sssssshhhhh." I whispered lightly, barely making any sound. Hardly touching him at all, I patted his back, barely moving, to let him know to be still and quiet.

But he couldn't stop. The whimpering was hardly audible, almost silent, but it was there, way back in his throat.

I prayed that the things couldn't hear him.

They sniffed at the driver's window, then moved to the cracked windshield, making sniffing sounds at the cracks.

I pressed as far back against the Pilot's roof as I could move, keeping my face out of the moonlight.

They climbed all over the Pilot, scratching and sniffing.

I held my breath, keeping my fingers in Hank's fur. He

sensed what I was feeling, or what I was thinking. Whatever it was, he got it, and the almost silent whimpering stopped.

We were both as silent as the dead.

I was sure his heart was slamming as hard as mine was, but both of us hardly breathed.

The reptilians continued sniffing and scratching. Through my fear, I was getting the distinct impression that their vision wasn't all that good. It seemed that they relied heavily on smell, sound and vibrations.

Hank and I remained still and silent, and we waited.

Finally, they moved away, scuttling off the pilot and skittering away in the snow.

We listened to their strange scratching sounds fade.

Then we stayed still and quiet for a while longer.

And then dawn seeped into the sky.

I WAS able to open the driver's side door, and I crawled out onto the snow. I thanked my lucky stars that I'd raided Luka's closet for the jacket and boots. There were warm ski gloves in her pockets, and as I pushed myself painfully to my feet, I dug them out and put them on. I hadn't needed them in the warmth of the Pilot before I crashed it, but now I did.

Hank followed me out, and we trudged through the snowy field and made our way back to the country road. He seemed no worse for the wear, and I thanked God for that. If he were hurt, I'd have to leave him. He was too heavy for me to even dream of carrying. And truthfully, I didn't think I could leave him. We'd both die in the cold.

Looking up and down the road, I guessed that this had

not been a well travelled road before the invasion, so I figured our chances of a car passing us were slim to none.

This could either be good or bad, depending on the type of people who might pass by. Judging from the way some people were acting in the midst of the chaos, I wasn't inclined to easily trust anyone anymore. I didn't think Hank was, either.

A wave of helplessness washed over me and I took a shuddering breath. It seemed an impossible thing, to survive the day again. I was cold, and exhausted, and my entire body ached.

But I had two choices: give up or move on. I wanted to stay alive.

Survival was the name of the game, by any means. This was a war, and there were casualties.

I'd do whatever was needed to keep Hank and I safe.

We continued on the silent road. He stayed close beside me, his head next to my arm. I could easily reach up and pat his head at any time, which I did every few minutes. Hank was all I had left in the world.

After a while walking, we stopped and I dug out a water bottle, pouring some water into a little plastic bowl I'd brought for him. We both drank a lot. The cold and the fear, the spikes of adrenaline, had leached us both of fluids.

I poured some dry dog food onto my glove and let him eat a few handfuls.

Then I dug out a banana I'd taken from the kitchen cupboards at the Doriga house. I ate that quickly, gripped the hammer in my gloved hand, and we moved on.

My eyes scanned the sides of the road, looking for any sign of a cabin or house where we could hole up for a while.

Snow shrouded the fields, and the tops of wheat poked through the surface, shivering in the wind.

I wondered how many underground tunnels lay beneath the snow, so close to where we walked.

Don't think about it. Keep looking for shelter.

Out here in the middle of nowhere, the pickings were slim.

I was cold and the wind wasn't kind, every so often tossing snow into my face and eyes. Hank dipped his head down and shook it, trying to rid his eyes and nose of snow. I worried about him. How long before dogs suffered damage to their paws out in the cold?

But we kept moving.

Finally, after a couple of hours of walking, I spotted a cottage set way back, up against the woods. A car sat in the driveway. The front door to the house was left open. That meant only one thing.

The reptiles had been here.

"Come on, Hank. We'll be safe here for a little while." My face was so numb with the cold that I could barely talk.

The air smelled of wood smoke. I hoped for a wood stove.

We walked through the snow, up to my knees and a fair way up Hank's legs. He did a kind of hop over the snow. Like me, his spirits seemed to be bolstered by the sight of the cabin, and the fact that we were heading toward it.

The garage door was open, housing a white pick-up truck, a beater, to be sure, but it might still run. It was parked haphazardly, like the person parking it had been drunk.

Or scared out of their mind and near hysterical.

Wind had driven snow in through the open door, but the cabin felt much warmer than it was outside. That meant there was still heat. Hank and I went cautiously in, and I shut the door behind us. The lights in the kitchen and living room were on. There didn't seem to be anyone home, but I needed to make sure.

I crept from room to room, Hank beside me. His ears were raised, listening for movement. His nostrils flared and he sniffed at the air. He let out a growl.

Someone or something was in the cabin.

I lifted the hammer, and we warily moved on.

The first bedroom was off the living room, and was empty. I searched under the bed. Nothing.

Slowly and quietly, we made our way to the next bedroom, which was off this one. The cabin wasn't that big, which would make searching it easier. However, it would also mean less hiding spots if we needed to hide.

Hank's hackles rose, and his growling grew louder.

It was daytime, so whatever was in there wasn't a reptilian.

"Hello?" I tried. A human might talk back. A deadie would come shuffling toward me.

And that's what happened.

The sound of feet sliding along the floor toward us made a chill shiver up my spine. But at least it wasn't a reptile. As long as I knew there was a deadie, I could deal with it. It's when you didn't hear them sneaking up on you that you were screwed.

"Here, deadie, deadie, deadie, deadie," I sang out, lifting the hammer higher. I stepped a foot into the doorway and saw him.

He had been about thirty when he'd died. It looked like he'd shot himself, but he had apparently missed his brain and the lower half of his jaw was gone. He was coming after me, but there would be no teeth to chew me with, if he caught me.

He likely hadn't died right away. He must've shot

himself in the day time, because the lizards would've heard the gunshot and come looking.

It was lucky there weren't any deadies within hearing distance of the gunshot. If he'd been alive, waiting to die when they found him, it would've made his death so much worse.

He wore a mechanic's uniform that said "Larry" on it, speckled in blood. It looked like he'd just come home from work. Larry had likely witnessed some pretty awful stuff before coming home.

I murmured. "That sucks, Larry."

Larry didn't make any sounds, other than his shambling feet. He no longer had any vocal cords. His arms reached forward and his hands opened and closed. He'd worn his long blonde hair in a ponytail.

I spotted the guitar leaning in the corner, and a notebook with a pen lying on it on the side table.

It looked like Larry had been writing a song.

"I'm sorry." I readied the hammer, waiting for him to move a little closer.

Hank began to bark at Larry, but moved backward as he approached. Larry was tall, six feet at least. But he was hunching over, and as he came toward me he leaned forward, which presented his forehead to me. I could reach it if I swung at an upward angle.

When Larry was just over an arm's length away I jumped up and swung the hammer with all my might and hit him with the claw, sinking it through bone and into his brain.

Larry went down, crumpling on the floor in a dead heap.

It was then that the stench hit me. Larry had emptied himself after the bullet took half his face off. "We need to get him out of here. I'd rather take my chances with the lizards than be subjected to this. There's no getting used to that smell."

Hank seemed to agree with me, sniffing at Larry and turning his head.

"Let's get to work."

I DRAGGED Larry by the legs, out of the bedroom. He was ripe, and I couldn't help gagging as I pulled him through the living room, avoiding the area rug and keeping him on the hardwood floor, which would be easier to clean. I had to stop and rest several times, stars popped before my eyes and my vision grew fuzzy.

Once I'd pulled Larry's dead ass outside and buried him as well as I could in the snow, I headed back, Hank close at my heels.

But looking at the long red streaks Larry had left on the floor as I'd dragged him out, I realized that my work wasn't done. I heaved a sigh and looked around until I found a Swiffer Wet Jet, which, as luck would have it, was equipped with cleanser meant for hardwood floors.

It took about a half hour and three Swiffer pads before the floor was perfectly clean of Larry.

But it gleamed. I was proud of myself.

I scrubbed the stains from Larry's suicide as best I could with a bucket, strong cleanser and water. He'd been sitting in a hardwood chair at the time, so it was really just the floor around the chair and the chair itself. The comforter on the bed was spattered. So I pulled it off and shoved it in a garbage bag, throwing it outside the door. I tossed the chair outside, too.

If Hank and I were going to stay here for any amount of time I had to make it livable, and blood and decomposing dead body gore was out.

I poured food into a bowl for Hank. I'd have to find some dog food for him somewhere, but until then, when his food ran out, he'd have to eat what I ate.

People food is not good for dogs. I'd seen a gorgeous, robust German shepherd go from being completely healthy to have a leaking liver and almost dying from table scraps. I shuddered to think what it was doing to us, all of those preservatives.

Maybe it wasn't the meteor dust creating flesh-eating zombies, but the preservatives and chemicals in our food.

I wouldn't be surprised.

Anyway, people food was not my top choice to feed Hank. I wanted to keep him around.

I'd been too busy trying to clean up Larry's drippings to notice much else about the inside of the cabin. But now that I could relax, meaning not fear for my life immediately, I started to take notice of my surroundings.

As I stood up, I looked around the kitchen. There were definite feminine touches in the room: a picture of a sunflower, dishtowels hanging on a rack with a daisy pattern on them, and beside the sink, a diamond engagement ring. Not a huge rock, but not tiny, either. The woman who lived here, Larry's fiancée, I thought was a safe assumption, didn't like to wear her ring while doing dishes.

My curiosity was piqued. I looked around the living room. On a desk near the huge window was a picture in a frame, with Larry and a pretty, smiling girl of about twenty-four. Her dark hair hung around her shoulders, and she wore a burgundy dress. Larry wore a black suit jacket. The picture must've been taken at a wedding, or some other function.

Where was she?

The door had been left open, so I was willing to bet that she'd been dragged out of here, kicking and screaming, like all of the other younger women had.

Her purse lay on a fluffy chair, like it had been tossed there before the event. I went over to it, feeling strange about opening it. Even though the woman was gone, it still felt wrong looking in her purse.

Strange for a girl who used to steal. But that was another story. Aside from the revenge steal from the bitchy cheerleader, who had most likely been taken by the lizards (and now I felt bad about taking her stuff from her locker), I never would've stolen someone's purse. I picked locks for fun, and never actually took anything from anyone. Except for the loaf of bread from the grocery store, that one time --- and the cheerleader's purse.

Even now, I only would take what Hank and I needed to survive.

I unzipped her purse and found her wallet, flipping it open to look at her driver's license.

Megan Lewis. She had been twenty-five years old.

Where are you, Megan? Where have those creepy things taken you?

Underground.

Was she still alive? How many other girls and women had been dragged underground.

I continued rifling through her wallet and felt an overwhelming sadness as I looked at the photos of what must've been young nieces and nephews. Kids no older than four or five.

I set her purse aside for the moment and sat on the couch, looking off into space.

Hank jumped up on the couch beside me and placed his head on my lap.

"Hey, buddy. How you doing?" I stroked his head, then leaned my head against the back of the couch. Now that my life wasn't in immediate danger, I felt the throb in my head from the car accident. My back ached, too. I'd likely jarred it when the Pilot had rolled.

Still, I considered it a miracle that I was alive and hadn't suffered any broken bones. And I was also thankful that Hank seemed fine. If he ached, he wasn't showing it.

"You're a tough guy, Hank. You know it?"

He let out a puff of air through his nostrils in response. He may be tough, but he was tired.

I knew the feeling. I closed my eyes, and thought about my sister Kelly. Had she been taken underground? There was a chance these women were still alive.

The thought of what the lizards could be doing with all the women they'd pulled into the ground send chills trembling through me. My eyes snapped open, and my heart began racing at the thought, and suddenly I felt like I couldn't get enough air.

Hank lifted his head and licked my hand, as if to say, *Take it easy, Zoe. Rest for now. Worry later. We can't fight and survive if we are exhausted. Rest now.*

I closed my eyes and forced my breathing to slow, and felt my heart slow in measures. I ran my fingers over Hanks back, and concentrated on the feeling of his fur beneath my skin.

WHEN I AWOKE Hank was licking my face. He jumped down and headed toward the door.

"It's that time, huh? Me too, actually." My bladder was full. By the way Hank was pacing in front of the door, I figured he needed to go worse than I did, and I really didn't feel like cleaning up any more messes.

I pulled my jacket on, wondering how much longer the heat in the cabin would last. It kicked on when the thermostat went below 68 degrees. I didn't dare turn it up. I wanted the heat to last as long as possible. There was a fireplace but I didn't want to risk drawing the attention of lizards or deadies with the smell of wood smoke.

I lifted the curtain on the window of the door and peered around. Nothing moved. So I slowly opened the door. "Careful, Hank."

He loped a couple of yards away and did his business quickly, then trotted back inside the cabin. Before I shut the door, I looked up at the sky, noting with growing trepidation, that the darkness was only a couple of hours away.

After closing and locking the door, I searched the house for hiding spots that wouldn't be death traps, in the unhappy event that the lizards found the cabin. They'd smell us, so if they kept searching until they found our hiding spot, I'd have to kill them quickly.

I'm small, but Hank is a big dog. I'd have to find a place that would hide us both.

The cupboard under the sink was out of the question. Hank wouldn't fit with me. I kept looking.

In the back bedroom, the one I thought of as Larry and Megan's room, was a walk-in closet. There was no lock on it from the inside, but then, if the lizards tried to open the door and found it locked, that would be a dead give-away.

Leaving the front door open might let them know that

they'd already come calling, but it would also leave more time to let our smell out --- and any wandering deadies in.

"Shit. I don't know what to do, Hank." I stared at the locked door. "Let's get to that later."

In front of the bed was a large trunk, which I figured held extra blankets. I opened it, anyway.

There were blankets. But beneath those, were guns. Lots of them. Guns and ammunition.

"Larry, you wonderful, paranoid son-of-a-skunk." Of course, since the invasion had taken place, I supposed he hadn't really been paranoid, had he? Something really had come to get them.

And suddenly I could see clearly what had actually happened. Larry hadn't killed himself during the day. He'd watched in horror as Megan had been dragged from the cabin, and he'd run into this room and shot himself. It had probably happened very quickly.

All those guns, and they hadn't protected him. It had all happened too fast.

The lizards probably weren't what Larry had in mind when he thought someone would come for him.

Imagine his surprise. I stared into the trunk.

Then I took stock of the guns. I didn't know what kinds they were, knowing nothing about guns whatsoever. I'd have to figure it out so I wouldn't shoot myself or Hank.

I picked up a small box and flipped the top open. Inside nestled a small pistol with a pink handle. Cute. This had to have been Megan's, though not necessarily. Maybe Larry liked pink.

Nah. It had been Megan's, Maybe an engagement gift? The gun looked as easy as point and shoot. It looked pretty much good to go.

"Good enough for now." I grabbed the ammunition that

lay in the same little box as the gun, and shoved it in my jacket pocket.

The plan was simple. Hide in the closet until daylight.

If something broke in and found us in the night, shoot it.

It was as good a plan as any, I figured.

And it was the only one I had.

HANK and I huddled in the closet at dusk. We sat way back, behind the clothes. The closet had apparently also served as a changing room. A mirror hung on one wall surrounded by press-on lights that you could press and have enough light to see how your outfit looked.

I thought I could risk having one of the tiny lights on. In the moment it took me to press on the little circular light, I caught a glimpse of myself in the mirror and almost shrank back, momentarily thinking the image was someone else in the closet with us. I didn't recognize myself.

I'd lost weight in the last three days. I doubted I even weighed a full hundred pounds anymore. Luka's clothes hung off me, and my face looked hallowed and drawn. My blue eyes looked too large and round for my face, and my hair looked like a tangled mess.

I dropped my gaze and moved back against the wall. If we lived through the night, I'd treat myself to a shower while there was still hot water. It had been three days since I'd had one, and the smell of my own sweat and fear was suffocating while we hid together, me sitting on the floor against the back wall of the closet, and Hank curled up beside me, with his head on my lap.

I trembled as we waited, and tried to keep my breathing

even. I kept the gun on the floor beside me, within easy reach.

The night was silent as I strained my ears to hear any sounds that might be a threat. Every so often Hank lifted his head and his ears perked up, and my adrenalin would spike, my heart drumming against my ribcage. But then he'd lay his head back down again and I'd breathe a quiet sigh of relief.

By the time we heard the birds chirping, signaling dawn, Hank and I were both shaken and exhausted. We crawled out of the closet on stiff and unsteady legs and I let him out. Daylight was bleeding into the sky, turning it from gray slowly to blue.

He followed me to the other bedroom, not the one Larry ate his gun in, and we both settled onto the bed.

After the night we'd had, I thought we deserved a nap on a real bed. "Just a few hours, Hank. Then we decide what to do next."

What to do next meant figuring out how to discover what was beneath the snow. Chances were that my sister was underground.

There had to be a way to find out if she was still alive. I couldn't live with myself if I didn't try.

And all of those other girls and women --- what would I do if I found them alive?

But my mind was as tired as my body was, and I could barely string two thoughts together. Just a little sleep, that's all I needed.

I closed my eyes and settled beneath the blankets with Larry's gun tucked under the pillow.

FIVE

When I woke up five hours later it was 11:15, and the sun was streaming through the thin strips through the blinds. I opened them enough to get more sunlight, but not enough for anything else to see inside.

The morning was quiet, except for the occasional bird chirping. There was no movement.

Feeling relatively safe, I refreshed Hank's water and poured more dog pellets in to his bowl. I looked in the cupboards. There were five large cans of soft dog food. The date didn't expire until the following fall. "You're in luck, Hank. Look what I found. There must've been a dog around here at some point. Maybe one that visited from time to time?"

Hank wagged his tail, then went back to chowing down. I found a can opener and added some of the soft food to his bowl. He ate the food with more enthusiasm than I'd seen him eat the dry pellets. "I'll see if I can get you more soft food, bud. We have to enjoy our small comforts where we can now. Times have changed. I'm going to take a quick shower. Hold down the fort."

I knew I didn't have to talk to Hank like he was a person, but it made me feel a lot better to talk to him. It made me feel like I wasn't all alone in the world. It helped staunch the fear, just a little.

There was still hot water. I kept the spray low, but cranked the heat of it as hot as I could stand it. The water felt like a massage on my sore muscles. Keeping my ears strained for any unusual sounds, I took my time sudsing up my entire body twice, a luxury I knew I couldn't continue, but one I felt I badly needed. Call it a morale booster. I washed my hair slowly, using more shampoo than needed. Rinsed, and washed it again.

I didn't know when I'd have a shower again. Anything could happen at any time. The soap smelled like cocoa butter, and the shampoo and conditioner like oranges, and by the time I stepped out of the bathtub I felt almost human again.

It was a strange thing to live in someone else's house. I kept feeling like Larry and Megan would come home and find Hank and I here, and wonder what the hell we were doing in their house.

Then I wished it were true, and that I'd just had a break down and that the world hadn't ended. We hadn't been invaded and the dead weren't rising and eating the living.

But this was how the world was now. There was no changing it, not any time soon. The best Hank and I could hope for was to avoid getting killed.

It seemed a tall order. But there it was.

The big, fluffy white towels felt incredible on my skin, and when I finished drying my body, I wrapped one around my head.

My clothes smelled funky, having been worn in for days. I searched the drawers and found fresh panties that were size small, and a sports bra that fit. The walk-in closet was taken up mostly by Megan's clothes. And as I looked through her stuff, I quickly realized that her size six jeans would be too big. Her shirts and sweaters, although a size small, would be roomy but fine.

I looked on top of the closet and found several pairs of older jeans folded up there. Size four. These must've been Megan's Jeans of Doom. Many women kept jeans from their high school and college years in hopes that they'd fit into them again. Or because they just couldn't bear to throw them away or donate them, because it meant that their bodies had matured. It's nostalgia. I understood, though I hadn't reached that stage yet.

The likelihood of being lucky enough to live another day was iffy at best, never mind another year or two.

Two pair of Levi's 505s. Two pair of 515s. Three pair of Levi's skinny jeans. I liked Levi's. The skinny jeans fit me perfectly. I put on a plain black t-shirt that was also folded on the upper shelf, and a sweatshirt from Megan's chest of drawers.

The fact Megan's clothes from earlier years were here led me to the assumption that this cabin had belonged to Megan's family. Perhaps it was given to her by her parents. Or she and Larry had taken it over.

I felt a pang of sorrow that she'd likely been dragged from her home, like so many others.

Maybe I'd find her.

If I lived long enough.

I TOOK the gun I'd chosen last night with spare ammo in my jacket pocket, my boot knife, tucked into the Uggs, and the hammer in my jacket. I pulled my mother's winter hat over my head. I pulled the windbreaker pants over the skinny jeans to cut the winter wind, and give just a little extra protection against the chill. I put on the ski gloves in the jacket pocket and flexed my fingers a few times, trying to get the blood moving in them. My hands felt cold and my fingers sluggish. I was still tired. The fear and shock of the last few days had wrecked me.

But I didn't have time to feel sorry for myself.

Suck it up. "Let's go, Hank. We're burning daylight."

We wandered through the woods, staying at the periphery of the trees. I didn't want to travel too deeply into the forest yet. This little jaunt was an exploratory trip, to see how close the reptiles were living to the cabin.

My body trembled as I looked the ground over. Snow blanketed the entire area. The snow had come again overnight, dropping another several inches on top of the foot that the storm had dropped on us. None of it had melted.

The holes could be anywhere. One wrong step and we could simply vanish through the ground.

I stepped lightly and carefully, and Hank did the same. He seemed to know what the point of the walk was, which didn't surprise me. He knew what the deal was.

My eyes continuously scanned the ground, the trees around us. Every few minutes I stopped, searching the snow for imperfections; dents, holes, uneven snow that would suggest a sinkhole. I didn't know if the reptiles covered the entrances to their underground structures or not.

If I had a slight idea how far underground the structures were, I could figure out more about how they were dug out.

But the only way for me to find out would be to find an entrance and to venture down into it during daylight hours. I felt secure in my theory that the reptiles couldn't take the daylight, which is why they never emerged after daybreak. Otherwise, it would be a free for all reptiles during daylight hours.

Instead, they were hiding underground.

What the hell was under there? Did they nest? Sleep? Where were the girls and women they'd dragged under there, kept separately from the reptiles or were they in the same areas?

I imagined what it would be like for those women. Cold, dark, barely able to breathe, if at all, with the alien monsters scuttling around. The thought sent a wave of terror washing over me, and a chilled sweat broke out over my back.

Hank moved nearer to me, nudging my hand.

"I'm okay, Hank." I kept my voice low, almost a whisper. "Just a little freaked out. But we can't just hide in the cabin, can we? We have to find out what happened to my sister. To Luka."

His ears lifted at Luka's name, and his eyes widened and searched my face.

I pointed to the snow beneath us. "She's down there somewhere. We need to find them."

He sniffed at the ground, then sat and waited for me to start moving again.

Suddenly he jumped up and turned around, snarling.

My heart froze. I turned.

A deadie stumbled through the snow toward us.

"Stay here, Hank. I've got this." I pulled off the ski glove and shoved it in my jacket pocket as I walked through the deep snow, still keeping my steps as light as I could, and pulled the claw hammer from my backpack. It was sticking out by the handle for easy access.

The woman had probably been in her sixties when

she'd died. Her white hair stuck out around her head in messy curls. Her eyes were milky white in her pasty face as she approached me, her hands reaching for me. She'd been on the heavier side, and in death she had trouble making her way through the drifts with her bulk. Her flannel nightgown billowed around her.

I swung the hammer back and hit her through the top of her head. She didn't drop. The claw stuck, but I was able to yank it out and hit her again, for good measure.

A high pitched shriek sounded to my left, and I looked up to see a boy of about fourteen heading toward me. He was considerably quicker and more nimble than the woman, and he climbed over the snow.

Hank snarled louder, coming up behind me.

"Don't bark, Hank. Okay?"

The hammer was stuck in the woman's head, and I didn't have time to fool with it. I shoved her away. No easy task. She was dead weight --- literally. She stumbled back, her eyes rolling, her dead brain puzzled by the sudden short circuit caused by the claw of my hammer.

I pulled the knife from my boot, but by then the kid was almost on top of me. His teeth were bared, blood and gore stuck between them. He made growling sounds, and came at me like he meant it. His swinging arms knocked the knife from my hand.

I jumped back, trying not to scream. The reptiles might find a way of pulling me under the snow if I was close enough to a sink hole.

The kid grabbed my leg and chomped down on my boot. I felt his teeth through the fake fur, and I hoped they hadn't penetrated.

I kicked out with the other foot and booted him in the head.

His head snapped back with the impact and he fell back on his ass, but he was climbing up by the time I began crab walking backwards. My mind screamed for me move faster, to get away from him.

Hank jumped at him from the side and knocked him over.

The dead kid began crawling after him.

Hank snarled and let out a warning bark. His fur stood up and he readied himself to attack.

If the kid bit or scratched him, it would be the end of him.

Then I remembered the gun. "Hey!" I stage whispered to the kid.

He turned to me and drooled.

I grabbed the gun from between my lower back and waist band and aimed for the kid's head. "Hank, stay."

Hank didn't like the command, but reluctantly sat down. His shoulders bunched, ready to attack.

The kid was so close now.

Hank growled and stood. He barked and started toward the kid.

I tried to pull the trigger but my finger wouldn't work. My finger was numb with the cold.

The kid grabbed the barrel between his teeth and chomped down. His finger found the trigger and the gun went off, the bullet whizzing past my head so close I felt it.

"Jesus Christ," I grunted. "You asshole."

I tried to move the gun so that the barrel pointed inside his mouth but he wouldn't let go of the gun.

My eye caught the shine of my knife blade in the snow. Letting the gun go, I bent down and reached for it, kicking my legs, pushing myself sideways toward it. My fingers reached it and curled numbly around the handle.

Lucky for me. If I'd grabbed the blade I could slice the fingers to the bone and not feel a thing.

The kid crawled toward me, the gun no longer in his mouth. His growls were now urgent and frantic with his hunger. Hank jumped on his back and the kid went face first into the snow.

I pushed myself backward, and then up onto my knees. "Down, Hank! Let me get him!"

Hank jumped down, his eyes unhappy about it.

The kid lifted his snow covered face and resumed stiffly crawling toward me.

In one swing I jammed it into his ear. His mouth opened he dropped sideways onto the snow.

I slowly stood up, panting. "Thanks, Buddy."

Hank came up beside me and pushed lightly against my leg.

The gun lay mostly covered in snow, but the black handle stuck out, a contrast to the pure white around it. I pulled the ski glove out of my pocket and pulled it on, hoping it would thaw okay. I took the other off and picked the gun up with that hand. It still worked okay --- the hand --- I didn't know about the gun.

I looked around, turning in a slow circle, my head whipping back and forth. The sound of the gun going off could attract deadies from miles around.

Hank growled, loudly, looking at something behind me.

"Oh, come on. This is getting old." I turned, holding the gun in front of me, getting ready to shoot if I had to.

Dark hair, hanging over caramel eyes. It was smiling.

Deadies didn't smile. Did they?

Then it spoke. "I heard the gun shot. Came up on you just as you skewered your zombie-kabob. Nice moves, chick.

But you almost got dead. Let me show you how to use that thing."

And I laughed, relief flooding through me.

He was alive.

And he had a crooked smile that made me want to smile even bigger.

Hank pushed between us, looking up at the kid to let him know he meant business.

The kid smiled at Hank and let him smell his glove. "Ryder, with a 'Y'."

A smile stretched the width of my face. "'Kay."

"Nice to meet you, Kay."

"No." I had trouble speaking. I wondered if my brain had gone numb or if I was having a stroke or something.

"No? It isn't nice to meet you?" He said, through the hair, one eyebrow raised.

I tried to explain through frozen lips. My speech was slow. I couldn't feel my face. "No, my name isn't Kay. I just meant 'okay'."

"Ah. Got it." Hank nuzzled his hand. "And you are?"

"Hank."

He looked up at me, his face quizzical. "Your name is Hank?"

This was getting painful. "No. He's Hank. I'm Zoe."

"Zoe and the zombies. I like it."

"Cool." I was at a loss for words. He was real. He was really real.

He patted Hank's head. "Good to meet you too, Hank."

I stood watching them with what I thought was a smile, but couldn't be sure because I really couldn't feel my face.

He looked up at me and chuckled. "Let's go, Zoe the Zombie Killer. I'll introduce you to my crew. We'll take the roads. You don't want to fall into one of their holes."

No. I surely didn't.

I SHOULD'VE BEEN MORE cautious of this new kid, who was about my age, but I wasn't. He could be a danger to Hank and me. A vulture, looking to take what we had and kill us after gaining our trust, but my instincts told me differently.

If he'd wanted to kill me, he would've done it already.

Still, it wasn't exactly prudent to blindly follow the guy wherever he led us.

"So, you've got some okay moves, but you're a little awkward, Zoe. It could get you killed." He looked at me and grinned.

"I'm a little new at this. Forgive my fumbling."

"And tripping. And falling. And dropping."

"Yeah, yeah." I rolled my eyes.

"It's okay. I'll help you. There are six of us at the compound. We have lots of food if you want to join us. We can always use another hand to help out."

"The compound?" There were many others? Amazing.

Hank seemed to like Ryder, once he'd decided that he wasn't a threat to us. He loped along beside me, seeming happy for the addition to our little team.

"Yeah. I'll explain it all to you. But the short version is, some doomsday preppers built the compound and stocked it with supplies, in preparation for some kind of apocalypse happening."

"You're kidding. I've seen doomsday preppers on TV. I thought it was all a little paranoid. But judging by what's happened, I guess not."

"I thought so, too. But I guess they weren't far off."

"I guess not. And if they are, thank God for the crazies." I gazed at the tree line set back from the fields, and again was struck by how gorgeous it looked.

The sun, now high in a clear, blue sky, reflected off the glittering snow and warmed us a little. It wasn't as cold today as it had been.

The wind shifted a little and I caught the scent of soap and shampoo off Ryder as he walked beside me. He wore a black winter hat over his hair, which pushed the hair on his forehead over his eyes. He used his glove to push them absently aside.

"Ryder, tell me what you know about those reptilian things. I call them lizards."

"We call them snakes, even though they have arms and legs. They are like lizards, you're right. But for some reason someone in the crew called them snakes and it stuck."

He glanced at me and I nodded.

"They live underground. You probably know that. You've likely seen them pulling women into the holes." He looked straight ahead and his face grew hard.

"I have. It's horrible."

"It's from a nightmare." He stopped and looked me in the face. "They took my sister. She's only fourteen years old. And I need to get her back."

"You saw them take her?"

"I had her by the hand as they dragged her in. But they didn't want me, so they did this to me." He held up his arm and shoved his jacket sleeve up, showing me several scabbed over gashes on his arm. "It was reflex. The pain made me let go. And then she was gone."

"They didn't try to eat you?" I thought of Jessica after she'd transformed. "One of them tried to eat me. She said she could smell my blood."

"She?"

"It was my two year old niece. Actually, she was close to three."

He dropped his eyes to the ground, his face sympathetic. "I'm sorry. It happened to my little brother, too. He was only ten."

"I'm sorry." I took a breath and looked around us. *Snow. Fields. Trees. And a seemingly endless road.* It did look like the end of the world. "I think they took my sister, too."

He gave a single, slow nod. "I was out here searching for holes. Trying to learn more about them. How they're spread out. How their lairs are built. Is that what you were doing? I saw you looking at the ground."

"Yeah. That's exactly what I was doing. I'm figuring they're nocturnal, because I haven't seen them out during the day, yet. Have you?"

He shook his head and looked out over the fields. "No. That's what we were thinking, too. They seem vampire-like. I saw them completely drain a kid I went to school with. Caught him in the middle of the street. He was trying to run." He shivered. "He was nothing but a husk when they were done with him."

A shudder moved through me. That's what the Jessica-thing would've done to me.

I frowned. "Why haven't they taken me? I was going to be eaten. Not dragged away. Once I'd gotten away from the one that used to be Jessica, they didn't try very hard to find me. I think they were leaving me for the clean-up crew."

He lifted his brows. "Clean-up crew?"

"The deadies. They eat what's left, don't they?"

He looked up and down the road. "Let's go. It'll be dark in a couple of hours."

We came to a side road and followed it for about a mile.

Ryder told me more about the snakes, as he called them, while we walked.

"They're aliens. I think they abducted the kids, did something to them so that they had alien DNA or something, then sent them back after they threw all those meteors at us. They're like some kind of hybrid now." He looked straight ahead. "Invasion of the body snatchers. For real."

"The news reports said that the dead rising had to do with the meteor dust."

"Zombie dust. Yeah. I don't think that was an accident, either. I think the bastards have been watching us for a long, long time." A gust of wind lifted his hair back from his forehead and face and I was struck by how delicate his features were. He looked almost elfish. High cheekbones and amber, almond shaped eyes. A straight nose. He was built lean, but he didn't look weak. His posture was straight as he walked, like he wouldn't back down from anything.

Maybe that's why he was a survivor.

"Zombie dust. That's exactly what it was. Do you think it's in us, too? Like if we die, we'll get up and start staggering around, trying to eat people?"

"Yes. I'm sure of it."

My stomach rolled. "Ugh. That is so disgusting. I don't eat meat."

He threw his head back and laughed. "That's the only reason it's disgusting? Not the fact that you'd be chomping down on human flesh?"

"Well, yeah. That too. But meat." I made a face. "Gross!"

He grinned at me. "Okay. If you die and get back up, I'll stab you in the eye. Put you back down. Before you get a chance to eat meat. I promise."

I laughed, and it felt good. I was amazed that I could still manage it. "Thanks, Ryder. I appreciate that. Is that your pick-up line?"

He snorted. "Nah. I have no pick-up line. But what are friends for? I'd expect no less from you."

"Oh, don't worry. I'll put a knife through your skull for you, too."

"Thanks, Zoe. That's the nicest thing anyone's ever said to me."

I laughed again, longer. "I guess this means we're friends?"

"I guess so." He gave me a closed lipped smile that made a dimple appear in his cheek.

"Good. Because Hank and I could use one. Right, Hank?"

Hank let out a puff of air behind us.

Ryder looked ahead of us and lifted his chin slightly. "There it is. Home sweet home."

I followed his gaze. A large structure with huge, metal squares spanning a huge expanse over a clearing sat at the top of a steep hill. "Wow. What is that?"

"That's the compound. It'll keep about anything out."

I looked at him, eyes wide. "Good. Because these days, there's lots of things that'll want to get in."

THE COMPOUND WAS BUILT of metal storage bins --- the big ones. They were stacked on top of one another, three stories high.

"This is incredible," I said. "How did you guys do this?"

"I had no hand in it." Ryder looked up at the structure, his face appreciative. "But the preppers did, a couple of years ago, I guess. That's what Kyle said. There are only a couple from his original group left. His wife, Sherry, and his brother, Ozzie. The others are stragglers. Like me. Like you."

"Who is your friend, Ryder?"

I spun around, freaked out that someone had been able to sneak up behind me. Meeting Ryder had momentarily lulled me into a false sense of security. I'd forgotten, just for a moment, how dangerous the world had become, and it startled me.

A tall, muscular man in his mid-thirties smiled at me and nodded hello. He looked at my face, his eyes narrow, deciding if I was a threat. It only took him a second, because then his grey eyes softened. He had a strong jaw and a slightly crooked nose, like it had been broken at least once.

"This is Zoe. Zoe, Kyle," Ryder said.

"Will you be sticking around, Zoe?" Kyle asked me. He seemed genuinely curious.

"Is that an invitation? I don't want to intrude." I wasn't sure how to respond to him. He was large and intimidating, but seemed to be okay with me.

He chuckled. "You're not intruding, Zoe. If I didn't want to offer you a place in the group, I wouldn't have."

"He really wouldn't have," Ryder confirmed. "I've seen him turn people away."

"You've turned people away?" I regretted the words as soon as they were out of my mouth. I didn't want to insult him. I needed a safe place for Hank and me.

Kyle's face grew serious. "They weren't nice people. Believe me. They were a threat to the group. They would've shot me in the head as soon as I turned around, then killed the others and taken over the compound."

I stared at him, my eyes feeling round in my face.

"You know that saying about tough times revealing who you really are? What you're made of?"

"Yeah. I've heard that.".

"Well, this invasion hasn't brought out the best in everyone."

That was an understatement. I remembered the carjackers out on the roads when Hank and I first drove out of town. "I've seen it. There were people torn from their cars when Hank and I left. I wanted to stop. Help them. But there were so many and . . . " A lump rose in my throat and I stopped, unable to talk. My eyes grew wet.

Kyle's eyes were kind and a little sad. "You couldn't have helped them, Zoe. You'd have been overtaken. You would be dead, now."

I pressed my lips together. Tried to swallow the lump down. The images of those families were vivid in my mind.

"So what do you think of our digs?" Kyle asked me, waving an arm toward the building.

I found my voice, though it cracked. "I think it's neat."

"Forty-foot steel shipping containers. Designed to carry 58 thousand lbs each. Can be stacked eight high. This is three high. The lower level has larger spaces. We've cut walls out of the containers to make a living area. Large enough to house a big group of people. There are lots of separate rooms on the upper levels. You can take your pick of the ones that aren't taken. That is, if you choose to stay."

I looked down at Hank. "Can my dog stay, too?"

"Of course he can. I love dogs." Kyle crouched down and held a hand out to Hank. "What's your name, big fella?"

Hank moved toward him, sniffing his fingers. He sat in front of him, tail thumping on the ground. Kyle couldn't be all bad if Hank liked him.

"His name is Hank. I found him alone in the house next door to ours."

Kyle's eyes flicked up to mine and held them for a moment. I could see that he'd already guessed, correctly, that I'd lost everyone. He moved both hands over Hank's large head, then over his massive body. "Well, it's lucky you found each other then, huh?"

"He's all I have." I said it more to myself than to anyone else.

Ryder moved a hand over the back of Luka's ski jacket. I had to stop calling it Luka's ski jacket. Luka's boots. She was gone. She may never come back. If she did, and we came across each other and she wanted her stuff back, I'd give it all back to her. But in the meantime, it was mine.

It was easier to think that way, now.

"So will you stay?" Ryder asked me.

I shrugged. Smiled. "Sure."

SIX

Kyle introduced me to his wife Sherry, a tall, sinewy black woman who looked like she didn't have an ounce of fat on her. She wore black leggings and her toned muscles were apparent under them. Her hair was held back in a thick, wavy braid. Her large, dark eyes smiled at me.

"Nice to meet you, Zoe." She had a strong, friendly voice.

"Thanks for having me," I said to her, not sure what else to say.

"Of course. Let's introduce you to the rest of the group, then we'll get you set up in your own room, okay?"

I nodded, suddenly feeling vulnerable and humbled by the kindness I'd found in these people. How could I be so lucky?

A tall but leaner, less muscular version of Kyle sat at a large metal table with a girl of about fifteen, and another boy of about twenty.

"This is Ozzie, Logan and Mina. Guys, this is Zoe. She'll be joining the group."

The crowd waved at me.

"Nice to meet you, Zoe," Mina said. She wore her dark hair in a boyish short crop. She was a natural beauty, with thick dark lashes and even features.

"Nice dog," Logan said, leaning forward and reaching a hand out to Hank.

I nodded my thanks. "That's Hank."

"I love dogs," Logan said, smiling at Hank and patting his head and back. "Hey, Hank."

Hank seemed to be smiling. His movements were light and cheerful. He'd found an actual pack to be a part of. So had I. What could be better?

Ozzie nodded. "Meetcha."

I nodded back.

"Ozzie is a man of few words, Zoe," Mina said. "A trait you may appreciate. As I do." Then she threw a look at Logan.

He looked up at her. "Oh, what? Like intelligent conversation isn't a good trait?"

She shrugged. "I don't know. Haven't heard any in a while."

He shook his head. "Go get her, Hank. She's a mean girl."

Mina laughed. "You love it."

"Yeah, yeah. Don't listen to her, Hank." Logan seemed to have fallen instantly in love with Hank, and the affection was definitely mutual. He rolled onto his back and offered up his belly to Logan.

"Come on," Sherry said. "Let's get you settled in and then you can have something to eat."

My stomach growled at the thought.

The upper level had rows of large rooms made from the shipping containers. I chose a room on the left. Each room had a three by four square cut into the wall for a window, covered in bulletproof plexiglass, which was covered in a steel mesh.

"Nothing is getting through those," Sherry said as I moved to the window and looked out.

"Pretty safe here, huh?" I looked out over the snow capped trees and fields. Were there lizard holes out there?

"Safe as we can be, given the situation." She walked up and stood beside me, then, as if reading my mind, said, "We haven't seen them come out of the ground around here. And believe me, we've been watching."

"Doesn't mean they won't, though."

"We've been out checking the ground during the daylight hours. It's almost supper so everyone is in right now. But they've been spreading out further and further over the area. We're trying to figure out why they haven't dug their little hidey holes around here."

"Maybe they will, yet." A quiver moved over me and I hugged myself. "I can't find my sister."

"They took my daughter." Her voice cracked. "She was only fourteen."

I turned to look at her. "Why have they taken the girls? What are they doing with them?"

Her eyes were misted over, and her face looked haunted at the thought. "We think they take girls and women who are the most fertile, so that they can breed them."

It was my worst nightmare. "Why don't they breed their own creepy females? Why do they need ours?"

She shrugged and shook her head. "We don't know. Maybe it's just part of the invasion. Infiltrating every part of us that they can. Maybe it makes Earth more habitable for them. Creating hybrids, like they did with the kids."

"Because the children were more pure. Not as many toxins in their bodies," I said.

"That's what we think," Zoe said.

"I can't believe this is happening." I was thinking out loud. Which I'd done a lot of since I'd found Hank.

"Believe it, Zoe. This is real. But as bad as it seems, having to deal with the chompers during all hours of the day, and the snakes at night, we still have a chance. It's not over until it's over. You're a survivor, that's why you're still here. You'll do well with us. We can fight them. We're learning more about them all the time."

"Like what?"

"Like they're allergic to UV rays. We have LED UV lights and we've tested them. Ozzie ran into a few out on the road trying to get back here last night. He lost track of the time trying to gather up as many as he could find."

"Oh, shit. What happened?"

"We'd already figured that they couldn't take sunlight, since they only come out at night. He had a bunch of the UV lights in the truck with him. As soon as the sun went down, they came out of nowhere and jumped all over the truck. It was his chance to test them out. It worked like a charm."

A tremor raced over me, remembering when Hank and I had been attacked the night before last. "They sure would've come in handy the other night. Same thing happened to Hank and me on the road."

"And you're still here to tell the tale. You're one tough young woman."

"Or just lucky as hell."

"Maybe you'll bring us all luck." She rubbed my shoulder as if it were a rabbit's foot.

I smiled. It was good to not be so alone in the world anymore. Just me and Hank in a world of monsters.

The sound of work boots approaching behind us made us turn.

It was Ozzie. "They shrank at the UV light like they'd been burned. Their skin started smoking and they took off like bats out of hell."

"Or snakes out of hell," Sherry said.

"Snakes from another planet," I said. "Right?"

Ozzie nodded once. "That seems about right."

"Does anyone know where these things even come from?" I asked them.

Ozzie shrugged. "Hard to say. Maybe someone does, somewhere. Or did."

"If we could figure that out, we might be able to figure out how to annihilate them. Like, in mass numbers." I felt a pleasant buzzing in my head at the thought.

Ozzie grinned, and Sherry straightened at the idea, her eyes brightening.

Nothing like the thought of mass *alienacide* to boost morale.

"If there's a way," Sherry said. "We will figure it out."

Ozzie nodded. "Let's put a pin in this conversation and go down to eat. I'm starved."

WE ALL SAT at the large table in the dining room/living room area. The place was utilitarian, with poured concrete over the floor of the shipping containers and the windows cut into the steel walls. It was like a large warehouse. All anyone cared about was that it was safe.

The smell of the food on the table made me weak with hunger. Fried chicken, biscuits and corn were dinner, and it was delicious. I closed my eyes and I chewed the crispy breading. I felt like I'd died and gone to heaven. "Mmmmm."

"Not bad, huh?" Kyle said, smiling.

"How are you guys able to do this? Food, cooking?" I was amazed.

"Over the last ten years, Sherry and I have stored enough food to keep us and a few friends going for over twenty years. We began preparing and storing back then, in the unhappy event of an apocalypse. That unhappy event happened."

"Just like we said it would," Sherry added, taking a bite of her buttered biscuit.

"Everyone thought we were crazy," Ozzie said. "Better crazy than dead, I guess."

"Or captured," Logan said, his face solemn as he sipped bottled water.

It seemed everyone lost somebody. Or many somebodies.

Was this something they'd foreseen ten years ago? Ryder had mentioned the preppers but I'd still been too dazed with happiness to find another living person at the time to have absorbed what he'd said about them. "Did you know it would be an alien invasion, complete with the added bonus result of the dead getting up and eating our friends and neighbors?"

"Honestly," Kyle began. "We didn't think it would be an alien-invasion-slash-zombie-apocalypse. We thought it would be an oil crisis. No oil to heat our houses, run our vehicles or the vehicles that bring food to the grocery store. Run planes, trains, ships. Pretty much throwing civilization into a clawing, murdering, survival-of-the fittest type mess."

"It wasn't oil," Mina said. "But they weren't far off the

mark in terms of the result. It is a clawing, murdering, survival-of-the-fittest mess."

"We also have a stockade of weapons," Ozzie said, pushing his clean plate away. "And we've trained. Kyle and I were marines. We came back from Iraq, but a lot of us didn't. We figured we'd prepare for the worst, because the worst happens when you're not prepared."

"That's for sure." I looked at Ryder, who was still working through his corn. He apparently wasn't a fan of it, but given the food shortages that were now upon us, he wasn't about to leave it uneaten. "Thank God Ryder found me."

He looked up at me and grinned.

"I'm sure you'll be a valuable part of our group," Kyle said. "You're not big, but you're obviously tough and resourceful. That's what we need."

"I'll do my best," I said. And I meant it. It was the very least I could do to pay back their kindness. "Hank will, too."

"Hey, never underestimate the value of a dog," Ozzie said. "I had a dog partner in Iraq. He helped save my ass more times than I could count."

Since there was no other dog around than Hank, and judging by the sadness that crossed fleetingly over Ozzie's face, I assumed that he hadn't made it back.

"What is the plan? What's the goal of the group?" I wanted to know what my purpose would be. It would help me feel useful and like I had a place in the group.

"The goal," Sherry said, "is to rescue our daughter, and any other females we've lost to those creepy-ass things, and then as many others as we can."

Kyle nodded. "Then we find a way to wipe them off the face of the planet."

I nodded, wondering how the hell we were going to pull that off.

Ozzie said, "It's a tall order, but we're in a war, Zoe. It's a simple concept. Search and rescue, then kill the enemy."

I gave a single, determined nod. "I like it. Show me how."

THERE WASN'T much time for training after dinner was finished. We all noticed darkness moving over the last vestiges of light beyond the windows. Each window had a sliding steel door which locked over the plexiglass, so that anything outside couldn't see in. Of course, it meant that we couldn't see what might be outside, either.

Still, it was better to keep a low profile.

There was a watch tower which could be accessed by a set of metal stairs, through a trap door in the roof. The tower was built directly over the trap door, so that going up into it and leaving it wouldn't leave the watcher vulnerable to deadies or lizards. Or snakes, as this group called them. I still thought of them as lizards, or reptilians.

Aliens are what they were. But for some reason the term terrified me even more than names like 'snake', 'lizard', or 'reptilian'.

Whatever kept me from going into a screaming, shrieking fit from which I might never return was good.

I was shown the watch tower by Ryder, whose watch it was for the first two hour shift. I sat in one of the chairs with him. The watchtower was covered in plexiglass and mesh, like the windows, but the mesh was thicker. Here, a watcher could see out pretty clearly but it was difficult for anything to see in.

I sat in a wooden chair beside him, and looked around the outside of the tower, which offered a 360 view of the outside around us. The tower sat about fifteen feet above the roof, so that it lent an excellent view of the ground.

Windmills sat about ten meters away from each other, and circled the compound. That was how the group maintained energy for the compound.

"How do you guys hook up to running water?" I asked. The bathrooms were just like they would be in a house, just more utilitarian. There were four of them. And the kitchen sink used running water.

"It's a pipe that runs down into Pine Lake, which isn't that far from here. It's just beyond those trees." He tipped his chin forward, toward the trees. "So far, it's worked like a dream."

"They really thought of everything, haven't they?" I was awed at what Kyle and Sherry had accomplished here. I'd seen compounds like this one on shows about end of the world preppers, but never imagined in my wildest dreams that I'd ever be living in one.

"Yeah. They have." Ryder said, leaning back in his chair so that it tipped back and the two front legs came off the floor. His work boots rested against the mesh in front of us. He rocked slightly back and forth, eyes watchful beyond the mesh. "Lucky for us."

He seemed amazingly calm for it being night time, watching for lizards.

"Have you ever seen any of those things around here?" I scanned the area, peering into the night.

"Nope. Not yet. But there's a first time for everything. We can't let our guard down. Here, take a pair of these." He handed me some goggles. "These are night vision. Anything moves out there, you'll see it. I like to use both. Toggle them back and forth."

He grabbed another pair from a small table beside him and traded his binoculars for them. I did the same.

I saw things moving out there and sat forward, my breath catching in my throat. "Oh, my God."

He chuckled. "Don't worry. What you're seeing now is regular wildlife. They don't eat the deer, rabbits, wolves, or fox. Anything like that. But a chomper will. You'll see those shuffling around. You can't mistake them for anything else."

"How can you tell the difference between regular wildlife and the lizards?"

"You'll know the minute you see one. They don't move like anything else."

That was true. I'd seen how they moved, up close and personal. I didn't ever want to see it again. But given the search and rescue plan, which I was on board with even though the thought scared me so badly it was paralyzing if I thought about it for too long, I knew that it was highly likely that I would see them again.

"I'd be putting the goggles on and keeping them on the second I got up here. I'd be so afraid to miss one of those things. They are fast."

"I use both the night vision and the regular binoculars. But whatever works for you, Zoe."

The guy was so laid back, I wondered if he had a regular pulse.

I spotted movement that didn't look like wildlife.

It didn't move like a lizard. It stood upright and walked slowly, hands held out ahead of them. Legs lifting high to navigate through the snow. "Ryder—"

"I see it." He grabbed a walkie-talkie from the small

shelf. "Ozzie. Kyle. Movement in the woods, heading our way. "Doesn't look like Zeke."

"Who is Zeke?"

"It's another term for deadie. Zeke the Zombie. But this doesn't look like a chomper."

"How can you tell?" I peered through the night vision goggles, watching as the figure climbed over the snow, sinking every now and then.

"Movements are too quick, too deliberate. But, there's a chomper about four yards from him. See it?"

I did see it. The deadie was moving slowly but surely toward what had to be gasping sounds. Whoever was trying to make their way through the woods in the dark had to be breathing hard, from fear and exertion. "Jesus. Is he nuts? The lizards will hear him. Or her. A person moves a lot quicker than the deadie."

Then Ozzie and Kyle were stealthily moving toward the woods, guns in one hand, something else in the other, but I couldn't tell what it was. "What are they holding there, besides the guns?"

Ryder leaned forward, peering through his night vision goggles. "Hand held UV lights."

The figure fell, and stayed motionless for a long moment. The deadie moved steadily toward him. "He doesn't know the deadie is following him. Should we yell to him?"

"No. We can't make noise. We don't want to attract whatever other chompers might be out there. One we can handle. A horde of them is a bit more difficult."

A flashlight beam appeared, moving over the trees. Then another. Whoever was wandering through the woods had to be able to see them.

The deadie did. It moved more quickly, stumbling toward the beams of light.

The figure must've heard the deadie coming. Moaning and screechy sounds deadies made when they get excited, because he began moving away from it, movements frantic.

"Help me! Help me!" It was a male voice.

"Oh shit," Ryder said. "He's going to bring every Zeke within a mile upon us."

The deadie turned and headed in his direction, away from the light beams and toward the screaming voice.

"This guy is an idiot." He spoke into the walkie talkie. "Guys, step it up! He might as well be screaming 'eat me'."

"I'll tell you what," Ozzie said, his voice crackling . "He don't stop screaming, I'll shoot him before Zeke gets to him."

"HELP ME!"

The figures of Ozzie and Kyle ran over the snow toward the screamer.

"Shut up!" Ozzie's walkie talkie was still on, his voice a harsh whisper. "Or I'll shoot you just to stop you from screaming. Are you stupid?"

The screaming stopped, and the figure moved toward the light beams, stumbling and falling several times.

"I got him," Kyle said.

I watched through the goggles as he reached the deadie and took it down with what looked like a knife to the head.

But now three more were moving through the trees toward them.

"Oh, shit," Ryder breathed into the walkie-talkie. "Guys. Three more heading your way."

Ozzie reached the figure and grabbed him, dragging him through the woods toward the compound. "Got him. Get Sherry to open the door. Mina and Logan to get this idiot in the compound."

When he was clear of the trees, he tossed the figure forward, sending him skidding on his knees into the snow. He hissed at the guy, "Go toward that building, moron. And shut the hell up. I hear another peep out of you, I'll kill you. Got it?"

The guy scrambled forward and ran toward the compound. Mina and Logan ran out to meet him and urged him forward, toward the door. They vanished below the roofline.

I lifted the goggles toward the woods, where Ozzie joined Kyle in stabbing deadies in the head. I lifted my gaze, scanning the woods beyond.

Five more shambling figures moved toward them.

"Ryder. They need to get out of there."

Ryder spoke into the walkie-talkie. "Five more Zekes. I think the idiot rang the dinner bell. You guys should come on back, before it really gets out of hand. We'll get them in the daylight."

But Ozzie and Kyle stood still, the fallen deadies slumped on the ground around them, looking around and waiting. They waved their flashlights around. Kyle's voice came over the walkie-talkie. "Which direction?"

Another four headed their way from the left. Three from the left, one from the right, and more figures slowly trudged their way toward Kyle and Ozzie's flashlight beams.

"Another four. All directions. Oh, Jesus. They're everywhere. Get out of there." Ryder's voice was panicked. "Now. For real, guys. Don't be stupid."

"All right," Ozzie said, resigned.

Ozzie and Kyle's figures, made green by the night vision, headed back out of the woods. Their movements were sure and effortless, as if they were used to moving around in the woods and snow in the black of night. I figured they'd been hunters before the invasion. Before they were ever marines. Now their game had expanded to include deadies and lizards.

"HELP! OH GOD! HEEEEEELLLLP!"

This was a new voice.

I lifted my goggles. Off to the left was another figure, heavier and larger than the last. He held a flashlight. The figure jumped forward, scrambling and falling over the snow toward Ozzie and Kyle's lights. He had to be at least twenty yards away.

"Oh crap," Ryder said.

Ozzie and Kyle turned around, toward the voice.

"HEEEEELP! They're coming!" The last word was punctuated with a long, terrified shriek.

"Holy shit. We're done." Ryder spoke into the walkie-talkie. "Shut that guy up, guys. You've got another pack heading toward you."

"Shut up!" Ozzie yelled, his voice echoing around the trees.

But the man kept screaming over Ozzie. Kyle ran toward the man, but the pack of deadies were almost upon him.

Then the man went down, a surprised yelp coming from him. The screaming started anew.

"Did a chomper get him?" Ryder's eyes were wide behind his goggles.

I strained my eyes to see through the goggles. They deadies were close but not on top of him yet.

Realization slammed into me and my stomach turned to ice, just as the man was pulled down, shrieking, into the ground.

Within seconds two lizards climbed out of the snow.

"Get out!" Ryder screamed into the walkie-talkie. "SNAKES!"

Ozzie and Kyle turned and ran, their movements like foxes moving through the snow, light and effortless. They navigated through the trees like they knew each one.

The deadies followed the sounds, heading steadily toward the building.

The lizards weaved around them toward Ozzie and Kyle. They skittered over the drifts toward them, covering the distance alarmingly fast.

There was no way Ozzie and Kyle would make it to the compound.

Ryder screamed into the walkie-talkie, "UV LIGHTS!!! UV!!!!"

Ozzie and Kyle had their UV guns on before they even turned around.

Through the goggles I saw Ozzie and Kyle fall backwards onto the ground, skidding along the snow, bringing their UV lights up as the lizards leapt at them.

The UV light hit the creatures in mid-air.

The most horrible sound I'd ever heard cut through the freezing night. Twin howls of agony and rage ricocheted off the trees, rising in the woods. The lizards smoked and disintegrated, green dust bursting outward like an exploding comet.

Ozzie and Kyle climbed back up and ran toward the compound.

Two more lizards emerged from the hole, skittering toward them.

Ozzie and Kyle were almost to the compound, but the lizards were closing the distance fast.

"UV!" Ryder screamed into the walkie-talkie.

Ozzie and Kyle spun, their movements as graceful as dancers and they hit the lizards with the UV light.

The lizards howled, shrieked, and burst, dust disintegrating over the white.

"Holy shit!" Kyle panted. "Holy shit!"

Ozzie whooped and let out a crazy laugh as he and Kyle turned back toward the compound, within seconds they'd disappeared below the roof line.

Ryder's voice was high with fear when he spoke again. "Jesus. There are more."

I lifted my goggles toward the woods and my heart froze as four more lizards headed away from the hole toward the compound.

SEVEN

Kyle yelled into the walkie-talkie for us to get back down into the compound. As Ryder pulled up the trap door two lizards crawled up and clung to the plexiglass, their strange, elongated feet sticking to it, their claws digging in.

"Go! Go! Go!" he yelled at me, holding up the trap door.

Hank was pacing frantically on the floor below. I climbed down fast but jumped the last four feet down onto the floor.

Ryder slammed the door shut and hit the four bar locks around it.

He jumped down and grabbed me by the hand, pulling me down the hall and to the steel stairs leading to the main level of the compound. Hank followed close behind.

When we got down there, the steel window coverings were slid into place and a black man of about twenty-five sat rocking back and forth, tears streaming down his face. "He collapsed. My dad. He couldn't go on. I told him to stay put and I covered him with branches. Said I'd get help. He must've woke up."

Sherry crouched in front of him, holding a steaming mug out to him. "I'm so sorry."

He covered his face and sobbed. "He had Alzheimer's."

Sherry placed the mug on the table behind the man. Moved her hands over his arms. She said nothing, but the horror she felt was all over her face. The old man hadn't known what was happening.

Ozzie and Kyle stood in the middle of the room, eyes scanning the windows.

"Shut up," Ozzie said, throwing the man a sharp look.

The man's shoulders shook as he cried silently into his hands.

Something thumped on the roof, then the scratching began. Claws scraping over metal.

We all looked up at the steel ceiling.

"They're on the roof," Kyle stood under the sound, staring at the ceiling. The black man lowered his hands, his eyes round with panic. "Those things?"

Ozzie looked at him as if he wanted to clock him. "Yeah. If it wasn't for you screaming your damned fool head off, they wouldn't be crawling all over us, and the Zekes, either. Idiot."

The man's face crumpled again. "I'm sorry. I was just so scared. For me, for my dad—"

"We're all scared," Kyle said. "But making noise like that draws the dead and the crawlers."

More thumping and scratching on the roof --- now the windows.

"Shit." Ozzie's eyes shifted around the room like those of a trapped animal.

"What are those things?" The black man asked, his voice thick with tears.

"They're aliens," Mina said, standing across from him. "They live in the ground."

"And they are not neighborly, asshole," Ozzie said.

"I already said I'm sorry," the man said. "And I got a name other than idiot or asshole. It's Wilson Brantford."

"Now's not the time for introductions, *Wilson*." Ozzie drew out the name, the same way one might draw out the words "Eff You".

Ozzie continued looking up at the ceiling, then down at the windows, gripping his UV light in his hand. Kyle stood still.

"I don't think they can see very well," I said, keeping my voice low. "I was trapped in a car I rolled the other night. Had two of them crawling all over the car, looking in, sniffing at the cracks in the windshield. But Hank and I stayed really still and they went away."

Everyone turned and looked at me, their interest piqued.

"Sorry. I forgot to mention that," I said.

"Good to know," Kyle said.

"I doubt it would've helped us out there," Ozzie said. "Zeke was after us, too."

Kyle nodded. "Yeah. It wasn't the ideal situation in which to test the theory."

"My dad might've been okay, if we'd known that," Wilson said, his voice low. He was thinking out loud.

"Your dad would've forgotten it as soon as you mentioned it," Ozzie said, softening a little. "I'm sorry, man."

Wilson nodded his thanks.

A part of me wanted to be mad at Wilson for leading the crawlers and deadies to us. But people react differently to abject terror. Not everyone can have grace under fire when the dead are walking, and they are after you to eat you alive.

The situation sucked. But chances were, the crawlers would've found us pretty soon, anyway. They came from a hole in the woods only meters away.

It would've been only a matter of time.

"That hole the snakes came out of, that was new, wasn't it?" Sherry asked. "If it had been there before, they would've come after us sooner."

Mina nodded. "I'd say it's pretty fresh. Maybe they dug their way out here over the last few nights. We're in the compound before dark. And it's pretty soundproof to the outside."

We all watched the ceiling.

"Kyle," Sherry whispered. "Turn off the lights."

"No," I said, softly. "Nobody move."

Kyle had mentioned that the place was soundproof and triple insulated. I hoped it would help keep the lizards from hearing or sensing us in the compound.

Hank curled up at my feet, his ears perked straight up, listening. I stroked his fur, comforting myself as well as him.

Everyone remained as still as we could, listening to the thumps and scratches late into the early morning hours.

They stopped all at once. The sudden absence of sound jarring.

That's how we knew dawn had finally come.

"I THINK they knew we were in here. If they didn't they know now." Logan looked miserable as he sipped coffee, staring down at the table.

Kyle and Ozzie pulled the sliding steel window covers

back, letting in daylight. They looked squinted through the windows, searching for movement.

"There's a few Zekes out there," Kyle said. "We'll need to take them down as quietly as possible. We don't need a horde surrounding the compound. We'll never be able to leave it."

"There were a shitload of them last night," Ryder said. "They must be around."

"Or wandered back off into the woods?" Wilson said.

"Let's get some food in us, first," Ozzie said. "Then we'll deal with them."

Sherry turned the lights off. "We need to plan the rescue mission." She turned to look at Kyle, her face haunted, and her eyes too large for her face. "We need to try and get Melody back. "Same with Marnie, Penny and Diane."

"And Kelly. My sister," I added.

"And Cassie," Mina said.

Susan nodded. "Absolutely. There's a reason those things took them. I'm sure they're still alive."

"Before they get to us," Ryder added.

Everyone was quiet for a moment, and I couldn't figure out if it was because everyone thought it would be a suicide mission or if they were trying to come up with ideas.

"Yeah," Mina said. "We can't just sit around waiting for them to figure out a way to get in here."

"Are they smart?" Logan lifted his tired eyes and looked around at everyone. "Or are they just driven by instinct, like snakes and lizards are."

"Oh, they're smart sons-of-bitches," Ozzie said, finally sitting down in a rocking recliner. He ran a hand over his face. "They orchestrated an entire invasion. Had this shit planned for years. Look at what they've accomplished so far. Gotta love that team spirit."

Kyle snorted. "Yeah. If the human race would've been so willing to work together, the world might've been a better place while it was still ours."

"It will be ours again," I said. "We just need to take it back."

A wide smile spread across Ozzie's face. "I like her, Kyle. She's got balls."

"She's right," Kyle said. "We need to take it back. And we will. We just need to figure out how."

Sherry put a pot of coffee in the middle of the table. "Well, we can't plan to take the world back on an empty stomach. We need coffee and breakfast. So, pancakes?"

Ryder smiled. "Pancakes, then counter take-over plans. Sounds good."

Wilson, who had remained quiet, merely looked around, hands wrapped around his mug. He seemed to be in some kind of shock.

I didn't blame him, but thought that he'd better snap out of it, and quick.

"Yeah," Ryder said. "Let's take it back."

Mina poured herself more coffee. "How hard can it be?"

LOGAN and I helped Sherry get breakfast ready. He fried bacon while I flipped pancakes. Sherry set the table and brought plates of pancakes out as I finished with each batch. Each of us got two slices of crispy, heavenly bacon. None of us were worried about hardening arteries, given the current state of affairs.

Logan's dark blonde waves hung over his face as he cooked, and I couldn't see the expression he wore.

"You like to cook?" I asked him.

"Not before everything happened. But it helps to have a task. You know? Keeps your mind off things."

"Yeah. I get that." I flipped pancakes over in the pan.

He nodded, and continued moving the bacon around in the pan. A few were burning.

"I love crispy bacon," I said. "Here, let's get those onto the plate."

"Oh, shit. Sorry." He lifted the bacon onto the plate I held for him. "I'm just a little freaked out from last night. You know? I mean, they know where we are now." He looked at me, his eyes frightened and his face pale. "They know."

I took a shuddering breath. "I know. But listen, we'll get them first. Okay?"

He looked at me, doubt and uncertainty on his face. "Yeah."

I gripped his arm gently. "Logan, we will."

He nodded.

"Now is not the time to fall apart. We need our wits about us. We've made it this far." I felt like a fraud. I was scared out of my mind.

"Yeah."

"Okay then. Let's go eat."

Breakfast was delectable, and even enjoyable. Everyone seemed to understand that we had to take things moment by moment, because we really never knew for sure what would happen in the next moment. It was possible that one or more of us could die today. The likelihood had become all the more real after listening to the lizards clawing all over the compound last night.

So we enjoyed the hell out of breakfast.

Wilson, who seemed to be coming out of himself in small measures, finally spoke. "I feel like I need to say something."

"Go ahead, Wilson," Sherry said.

Ozzie glowered at him. "Yeah. By all means. We're all ears, Wilson." Apparently he was still a little sore at Wilson for making such a racket last night. But I was betting he was more afraid than he was angry. Anger is just easier for some of us to swallow than fear.

Wilson shot Ozzie a look, then looked down. "First, I am sorry, for bringing the deadies and those alien things to your safe house. If it weren't for me and my dad screaming, they wouldn't even know you were here."

"Well, we don't really know that," Sherry said. "I think they were on the verge of discovering us. Those holes weren't out there a day ago."

Kyle nodded. "A bunch of us check the perimeter each day, man. It was just a matter of time. I think you just quickened the process a little."

"It was going to happen anyway," Mina said.

"Still. I'm sorry." Wilson looked at Ozzie. "Ozzie, you have every right to be pissed. You work hard each day to keep your people safe and I . . . I messed that up pretty good."

Ozzie studied him over his mug, took a long swig, then placed the mug on the table in front of him. "All right. I got it. But now that you *have* screwed it up, I expect that you'll work your nuts off to help keep us safe from here on out. That includes killing Zekes and the exploratory expedition we'll be embarking upon today."

"Today?" Wilson looked at him, wide-eyed.

"Yeah, sweetheart. Today. And you'll have our backs. Because I won't rescue your ass again. Savvy?"

Wilson slowly nodded his head, but his mug of coffee had begun to tremble slightly. "Yeah. Sure. I've got your backs."

When the dishes were stacked and washed, we got down to the first bit of business.

Which was to kill some deadies.

THERE WERE six deadies wandering around the entrance of the compound. They must've seen Kyle and Ozzie run back into the building. We saw them through the window facing the front area outside.

"You ever kill any deadies, Wilson?" Ozzie asked him.

"Just one. My girlfriend. It was by accident. I hit her in the head with a cast iron frying pan. I was in the kitchen when she came at me. It was on the stove, the closest weapon at hand." He looked momentarily sick. "I had to hit her a few times before she went down. But I didn't mean to kill her. She just kept coming at me. Trying to bite me."

"Same technique," Ozzie said. "But use a knife, hammer, screw driver. Something that'll penetrate easily. We don't use guns unless we have to, it draws more of them." He handed Wilson a screw driver. "This will do fine. Get them in the eye, the ear, anywhere you can reach the brain. You have to kill the brain. Get that?"

Wilson nodded, looking scared and nauseous at the same time. "I can't believe I'm doing this. We were going to get married this summer. I just started a new job. Now I'm about to stab walking dead people in the eyes."

"Stop your whining, asshole. Your plans have changed.

Roll with it." Ozzie unlocked the door and got ready to slide it open. "Everyone ready and steady?"

Everyone responded in the affirmative. Most of us merely nodding.

I gripped my claw hammer, claw pointed outward.

Kyle tipped his head down, gripped his hunting knife and said, "Let's get 'er done."

Ozzie grinned like a maniac. "Let's show them some love."

He pulled the door open.

And faced a crowd of deadies standing at the door, all standing docile, heads hung, as if asleep.

A moment after they heard the sound of the door sliding open, their heads lifted, one by one, and they began moving forward, hands clawing toward us, faces in various levels of decomposition. Their teeth gnashed and clicked as their scratchy, unearthly screeches rose. They moved frantically at us, trying to get to food.

There had to be twenty or more.

Kyle tried to slide the door closed, but it was too late. The dead were coming through it, falling and climbing over one another to get inside.

They were in, and there was no hope of getting out the door with the wall of dead coming at us.

Logan was pushed down by the dead as one of them fell on top of him, biting and tearing at his arm. His screams rose, shrill above the screeches of the dead. Blood spurted outward from his arm, bathing a deadie as it fed on him.

Hank barked wildly behind us.

My blood turned cold and the flight or fight instinct screamed at me to run.

I fought against it and swung the claw hammer into the

head of the deadie feeding on Logan's arm before it took another bite. "Help me get him out!"

Ryder and I each pulled one of Logan's arms and he screamed, high and long as one of the dead took a chunk out of his thigh.

Ozzie shot it in the head and it fell. He kept shooting. There were too many to stab. Kyle's gunshots joined his as they worked to kill the Zekes.

We pulled Logan back, and Sherry and Mina immediately set about trying to stop the bleeding.

When I turned back toward the door, more dead were climbing over the fallen. I struck one after another, swinging and yanking the claw out of dead skull after dead skull.

Ozzie and Kyle shot at their heads. They fell one by one, and more started climbing over the fallen dead. It seemed impossible to keep up.

"Back up!" Ozzie screamed. They'll get your legs!"

We all ran backwards, Ozzie and Kyle shooting one deadie after another.

"GUNS!" Kyle screamed, shooting every zombie head within site.

Dropping my hammer to the floor, I grabbed my gun, aiming at every dead head within my sights. But I kept missing. I'd get the throat, shoulder, or chest.

Forcing myself to focus, I shoved away my fear, and began hitting them in the head.

I heard guns going off behind and beside me. My ears popped and all sound went away. Everyone in the compound was shooting, trying to keep up with the dead.

Then I heard Ozzie cackle like a maniac, the sound muffled in my nearly deaf ears, and saw his hand jerk as he pulled the trigger on his pistol again and again.

One deadie squeezed through, falling over the pile of Zekes and fell over them, to the floor.

I continued shooting at the ones closest to us.

"Back up!" Kyle screamed. "Back up, we'll get trampled!"

Again, we backed up.

I was so focused on shooting the oncoming dead that I forgot about the one that had squeezed through. By the time I saw it, it had pushed itself to its feet and was lurching toward me. I aimed my gun but I didn't have enough time and it fell on top of me. It gnashed its teeth, screeching in my face as I pushed against its dead chest. This one had been a woman, and I was pushing against her once ample breasts, which now hung and felt squishy and loose beneath my hands.

I screamed, and suddenly she fell on top of me.

Someone kicked her off me.

"Sneaky one." Wilson grabbed my hand and pulled me up.

"Thanks," I said.

"The least I can do." He went forward, his face a study in determination as he stabbed a deadie in the eye, dropping it in front of us.

They were in the compound. Although there weren't as many moving, it was terrifying that they had breached the safety of the building.

Ozzie and Kyle shot the ones moving straight ahead while the rest of us got the ones moving forward from the sides. They were crawling over the ever growing pile of dead.

The pile began to spill forward, further and further into the compound, and the Zekes climbed and crawled over them to get to us.

Finally, Ozzie shot the last two.

For a long moment, there was no sound except for the heavy breathing of everyone as our adrenalin levels began sinking back to normal. We all had the adrenalin shakes, and each of us stood there quaking, lifting our gaze over the pile of dead and toward the woods for movement.

"Oh, shit." Wilson said, looking straight ahead, eyes widening.

We all followed his wild gaze.

Breaking from the shadows of the trees, more figures shambled forward.

"THERE ARE A FEW COMING," Ozzie said. "Must've heard the gunshots. Let's take care of them before we get another horde. I can't do this all damn day."

We climbed over the dead, our feet sinking into rotting backs. Organs spilled out, stinking like nothing I'd ever smelled before. I gagged, but kept going.

Don't think. Just do.

I fell onto the grass and launched myself forward, following Ozzie and Kyle.

There were about fifteen more coming through the tree line.

Ozzie got there first, and began stabbing, followed by Kyle.

I headed for a middle aged man in a grey suit, which still looked surprisingly clean and unwrinkled. He must've recently died, because other than the stupid, glazed look in his eyes and the unnatural, jerky movements as he quickened his pace toward me, he looked pretty normal.

Anyone could mistake him for one of the living and ask

him for help. Especially a child, who wouldn't know until the deadie was way too close that he wasn't alive, and meant to sink his teeth into you and rip out your flesh in chunks.

Rage overtook my fear and I jumped up swinging. I smashed the claw into the top of his head. The claw made a satisfying crunch as it sunk in, and the suit fell sideways.

Mina gripped a long, nasty looking knife with a thick blade between her hands and brought it down on the forehead of a teenage girl with half her face and much of her belly missing. Someone had done some chewing on her.

What a horrible way to die.

Ryder held a fireplace poker in two hands and did a running jump, jamming the poker through the eye of a large man in a police uniform. "This guy gave me a speeding ticket last week! He was a total tool!"

Kyle looked back at him as he pulled his knife from a dead woman's ear. "Yeah. That's Teddy Picket. He's been a bully since the first grade. But Ozzie knocked one of his teeth out for him in tenth grade."

"Way to go, Ozzie," Mina grinned, wiping her knife free of deadie blood.

"He took my chocolate milk." Ozzie came walking toward us, shoving his butcher knife into his tool belt. "That just ain't right."

Sherry climbed off a woman in yoga pants and a pink tank top that read, *M.I.L.F.* "Funny, I knew this one too. So did Kyle. She stole him away from me senior year of high school. For like a day."

Kyle looked over at her. "Wow. Gail. She looked good for her age, though."

"Yeah?" Sherry said, booting Gail in the dead head. "Not anymore."

"Aw, baby, nobody compares to you. I came to my senses, didn't I?"

"Yeah, good thing for you, Mister." She patted his cheek and looked back toward the compound. "Ah, Jesus. Look at that mess."

"We'll clean it up, baby." Kyle looked back toward the trees. "Once we're sure no more of the Zekes decide to be neighborly."

The scene was surreal. It felt like homicide cops at a murder scene in a movie, using humor to temper the horror.

This is what the world had come to. It's how we'd get through what we had to do to live.

"I'm going to go check on Logan," Sherry said. "He got bit pretty badly on his arm and thigh. They tore right into his muscle. I tied the wounds off tightly, but I don't know if the bleeding stopped. He needs painkillers and antibiotics."

"I'll come with you." Mina followed Sherry back to the compound.

A shudder moved over me as I remembered the dead biting into Logan, like he was fried chicken. And I felt my stomach turn over.

Taking a deep breath, I turned back toward the woods and caught Ozzie looking at me.

"It's happened before and it'll happen again, Zoe. We get used to it but we don't have to like it. We just have to keep going, any way we can."

"I know."

"It's okay to be scared," he said. "We're all scared. Gotta keep moving through the fear. You're doing fine."

For a long moment, we all stood watching the tree line as our bodies trembled and our hearts slowed, and our breathing stopped coming out in little gasps for air.

EIGHT

Ryder, Ozzie and I spread out along the perimeter and kept watch while Sherry and Mina kept an eye on Logan. Kyle and Wilson took a trip to town for fencing. We needed to keep the deadies out. As evidenced by the morning's events, they were becoming a real issue.

Mina came out and headed toward me. She'd put on a light blue parka with fur around the hood. She could've been a model in a catalogue, selling that parka. Pretty in a girl-next-door way, with even features and creamy skin, she didn't look like she fit in this nightmare. I wondered what her life had been like before the invasion.

Standing beside me, she let out a long breath as she looked around. "It's weird. All those people were just normal citizens a few days ago."

She was referring to the dead that had come out from the woods.

"I know." I lifted my shoulders and shivered. Even with the warm ski jacket, I was cold.

She grinned. "You don't talk much, do you?"

I looked down at the ground, and kicked at the snow absently. "I guess not."

"So who were you before this all happened?"

"Not someone you'd hang out with." I risked a glance at her.

"Now, how do you know that?"

I shrugged. "You look . . . nice. Like you come from a good home. People who cared about you. I'm a little rough around the edges. I might've done your hair, but that's the only way I think we'd have ever had a conversation."

"Ah, you're pre-judging me. Judging the book by its cover."

"You mean you're not nice?"

"Oh, I'm nice. But I've got all kinds of friends, from every walk of life. Well, had all kinds of friends."

"You look like a kindergarten teacher."

She laughed. "I worked at the gas station down the road. You were a hairstylist?"

I nodded. "I was supposed to start an internship. I'm pretty good, too. I think it really was my calling."

"Nah," she said. "This was your calling. Kicking chomper ass and figuring out a way to get our planet back."

The idea hadn't dawned on me before she'd said it. But maybe she was right. Maybe that's why we'd survived.

OZZIE, Kyle and Wilson had piled the dead onto a dump truck that had been parked behind a huge barn behind the compound. They were piled into the back, driven about a mile up the road, and dumped into a ravine. Hopefully they would be frozen for a couple of months if the weather cooperated. Then, they'd thaw and stink to high heaven. We thought of burning them, but no one could stomach the thought of what human flesh burning would smell like. We just couldn't do it.

I heard the sound of hardened snow crunching beneath boots. I turned to see Mina approaching. She'd gone back in about an hour before.

She looked troubled.

I thought of Logan. "How's the patient?"

"He's hanging in there, but it's bad. Really bad. Sherry is keeping him under morphine for the pain."

"He knew this would happen."

"What do you mean?"

"This morning, while we were doing dishes, he was scared. I gave him a pep talk. Now I feel like an asshole."

"Zoe, maybe it was the fear allowed this to happen."

I frowned. "We're all scared, Mina."

"Yeah, but maybe he hesitated. You hesitate, you die. It's like Ozzie said, you have to work through the fear. Use it, even. To give you an edge. Maybe he was paralyzed by it."

I said nothing, and looked toward the woods. I didn't feel comfortable blaming the victim, but maybe she had something there.

She changed the subject. "Do you want to swap for a while? Sherry has chicken noodle soup and turkey sandwiches on the table."

I hadn't even realized I was hungry until she mentioned the food. "Sure. If you don't mind."

"I don't. We all have to do our part around here. That means that we all need to do every job, and swap jobs when we have to. I can use the air. I mopped the floor where the deadies piled up." She made a face. "It was so gross. Organs that had fallen out. Blood that had gone bad. I had to have a bucket near me. I puked twice. Gagged when I wasn't puking."

My stomach rolled just thinking of it. "That's nasty."

"You don't even know."

A rumbling sound made us both turn toward the road. Kyle's big pick-up stopped in front of the compound. Wilson followed him in an H3 Hummer and parked beside him.

"They got the fencing. Good." Mina's breath came out in puffs of fog as she spoke.

"Nice ride. Wilson rode down with Kyle, didn't he?"

"Yeah. He must've picked that up during the trip. Good taste. That sucker is tough."

Ozzie came out of the compound and walked around the back of Kyle's truck. He patted the H3 on the hood. "Now that's what I'm talking about."

"It was sitting in the parking lot of a GM dealer. We broke the glass and found the key. No one there to respond to the alarm. There are a few more in the lot. We should make a trip back there and get at least one more."

Ozzie gave a nod. "H3s will come in handy." He turned his attention to Mina and me. "Any sightings of anything that shouldn't be near us?"

I shook my head.

"Nope. Not yet." Ryder walked toward the truck. "Need some help?"

"Could always use it," Kyle called out. He looked over at Mina and me. "You two keep watch until we get this unloaded. After we've all eaten lunch, we'll start putting it up. I want this area fenced off before dark."

So we would lose another day, working on the fencing instead of rescuing the women we loved from the crawlers. "We won't search for entrance points in the ground?"

Kyle stopped and walked toward me. "I'm sorry, Zoe. I have a daughter out there. But we have to get the fencing up or we could get overrun again. I have to keep our group safe. It's number one priority."

I swallowed down anger, which burned in my throat like lava. "Kyle, one more day could mean the difference between life and death for the women underground."

"If we die because of a zombie horde, none of it matters."

I knew he was right. But the urgency and desperation I felt brought tears of rage and helplessness to my eyes. I pressed my lips tightly together and tried not to cry in front of him.

"I'm sorry. I don't want to lose anyone. Do you understand that?" His face was kind, and his eyes held sympathy, which pissed me off because it made me want to cry all the more.

I nodded and turned back toward the woods.

He hesitated, and I could feel his eyes on me, then he turned and headed back to the trucks.

I gritted my teeth, staring out at ground around the trees.

"Zoe," he called to me.

I turned.

His head was tipped slightly to the side and downward as he looked at me. "Go get some lunch. Take a short break."

Saying nothing, I headed toward the compound.

I WAS heavy hearted as I sat at the table with a bowl of Sherry's soup in front of me. It was hot and tasty and warmed me as I listened to Logan's fevered cries from the back room. I heard Sherry's soft voice as she spoke to him, but couldn't hear what she was saying. Again I thought of the pep talk I'd given him about being survivors. Then this happens to him. I felt like a liar and a fraud, because my words, meant to give him strength and courage, had done him harm.

The soup in my bowl was cooling and almost gone when Sherry came out of the room. "I think he's asleep, for the moment. I gave him a sedative."

"Do you think he'll make it?"

She shook her head, one hand rubbing the back of her neck. She looked exhausted. "I don't know."

"You speak like a doctor. Are you a doctor?"

"I was. Had a private practice down in Glendon. Before all this."

"You still are." I nibbled my turkey sandwich. The bread was soft and still warm from the oven. Sherry made incredible bread. "You could've been a cook. This is excellent."

She offered a small smile. "Thanks, Zoe. I do what I can. You know?"

I nodded. "I do."

She sat across from me at the table. "You're still upset. Is it because of the Zekes? They were a surprise to us all. We hadn't seen a horde like that since we got here."

"Partly. But . . . " I didn't want to sound like I was complaining to her about Kyle. I definitely didn't want to step on anyone's toes.

"But?" She watched me, a question in her dark eyes.

"I just wish we could go get my sister from down there, where ever they have her. I don't want her to spend one more minute under there." I shook my head. "I feel like we're running out of time to save these women. I'm sorry. I don't mean to complain. I'm just really scared for them."

Sherry nodded. "Me too, Zoe. My daughter is down there. Ryder's sister. Ozzie's girlfriend. Mina's girlfriend."

"Her girlfriend?"

Sherry tipped her head. "Yes. Her partner. You know. . ."

"No, I get that. I'm curious why the crawlers took her girlfriend and not her."

"I think Mina was at work at the time. She stopped at the pharmacy to get a script filled." A worried look crossed Sherry's face. "She's a diabetic. I hope we can keep her in insulin for a while."

A light went on in my head. "That's why she wasn't taken. She is defective."

"I wouldn't put it that way," Sherry said.

"That's the way it was put to me, by my niece before she was completely transformed into a crawler. She said they couldn't use me because I'm defective."

"I had cancer," Sherry said. "Of the uterus. I'm in remission." She studied me for a moment, looking like she didn't really want to ask me the next question on her mind. "What makes you defective?"

I shrugged. "I honestly don't know, and since the invasion, I can't just go to the doc and ask for some tests. It's anyone's guess what's wrong with me. Other than fearing for my life I feel fine." I gave a humorless snort. "*I feel fine*. That's what a lot of people say just before they drop dead, isn't it? I should be so lucky."

Sherry pushed me lightly. "Stop. We need you here. We'll figure something out for you. Find a facility with working equipment or something."

I pushed out a breath. "Sherry, why aren't we going

down there? We may never have another horde. Or at least, not tonight. Isn't it worth the risk to get them back?"

Sherry studied me with big liquid eyes. Her coffee colored skin was almost ashen today. She looked sick with worry and beyond exhausted. "Not if we lose everyone. Yes, my daughter is more important to me than the group. Than —" her chin trembled and her voice cracked. She took a breath. "Than anyone. And I can't stand the thought of her down there." She swiped at a tear and I felt terrible bringing it up. "But we need a safe place to bring her back to if we manage to get her out. If we manage to get all of our girls out. What good is it if we get them out and the compound is overrun with the dead? We'll all die."

What she said made sense. But my heart disagreed with the decision.

She saw the doubt on my face. "Zoe, we'll go at first light. I promise. Okay?"

First light seemed like an eternity away, even as the sun sank ever lower in the sky.

ALL BUT SHERRY helped to get the fencing up. It was in sections, which helped. Kyle had owned his own construction business, and he had all the right machinery to drill holes deeply enough into the frozen ground to keep the sections of fencing from coming out.

It took us until dusk, but we got all of the sections in surrounding the immediate perimeter of the compound. The fencing was a good choice. Iron, with pointed peaks separated by only a foot. The fence stood six feet high, and had iron bars which stood vertically. There were no bars set horizontally to get a foot hold, other than one set across each section which sat about six inches from the ground. The dead wouldn't be able to climb over it, and if they did make it, they would impale themselves on the sharp points.

"Everyone in the compound," Kyle said. "Dark is coming."

Dark came and we ate leftover soup and sandwiches with only LED lanterns to light the room. We ate quietly, and listened for the tell tale sounds of the lizards as they climbed all over the compound, scratching and thudding on the windows and roof.

Within a half hour, we heard them.

We took turns keeping watch in two hour intervals, to make sure none of those things didn't find a way in while we slept.

Every so often Logan would cry out when the morphine would wear off, and Sherry, who slept beside him on a cot would quiet him down. His fever hadn't broken, and Sherry kept the pain and infection away as well as she could. His wounds weren't healing. Nobody knew what to do, except to try to keep him comfortable.

I slept fitfully, and volunteered to keep watch at 2:00 a.m. I was awake anyway.

It was hard to sleep with all the clawing and scraping all around us.

A dark thought crept into my mind, making my skin break out in gooseflesh.

Right now they couldn't get in. But what if these things figured out a way to drive us out?

TODAY WAS THE DAY.

We were going underground. I was beyond scared,

jittery, tired. My muscles ached from lack of sleep, but I wanted to get Kelly back. Today we were going to bring our loved ones out of the deep, dark tunnels they were in. They had to still be alive. We'd get them back. One way or the other. At least we would try.

We started with what we knew. We knew where one of the holes to their underground lair was. Ozzie spray painted a red "X' on the tree directly behind it, so we'd know exactly where the hole was located.

"But they've likely dug more tracks down there and made more holes to creep out of. They're probably scattered all over this place, now." Ozzie pulled his black winter hat over his head. His face looked even more angular with the hat on, and it reminded me of the wrestlers Derek used to watch on television every Sunday.

Kyle spoke, his hand on the door handle, ready to slide it open. "Walk softly and quietly. We know these things don't come out during the day, but that doesn't mean they can't. Keep your eyes open for any part of the ground that looks like it might be sunken in. Use your sticks to test the ground in front and around you."

We all had long sticks that Ozzie had found on the ground for us. Kyle and Ozzie were much more careful now about letting people wander outside of the relative safety of the gate. We were always waiting for the other shoe to drop. For one of us to vanish into the ground, or be torn apart by a silent deadie.

Moving as stealthily as we could, we followed Ozzie and Kyle out into the wooded area surrounding the compound.

When we approached the hole in front of the tree Ozzie had marked, we all slowed and lightened our steps.

We all stood, silent, around the hole as Ozzie set his

laptop on top of the laptop bag. He plugged the USB end of a long, coiled length of black cord. "Good thing I used to be a plumber before the shit hit the fan."

I lifted my eyebrows. I didn't know how a laptop and a long length of black cord were related to plumbing.

He caught my look and chuckled, and held up an end of the cord that looked like a mini flashlight. "This is an inspection scope camera. It takes pictures and videos, and it also does live feed. It's used for inspecting toilets, sewers, even vents and the inner workings of cars. It's great for all kinds of work."

"Including spying on alien life forms that have invaded the Earth," Ryder offered.

"Exactly," Ozzie said. "It's waterproof, so the snow won't bother it. It's ten meters long, so we can drop it down and keep feeding it through for a while, see what they've been up to without going down there half cocked and getting ourselves killed."

"That's a good plan." Mina crossed her arms over her chest. "Especially the not getting killed part."

"We can see where the women are," I said. I shivered. The air was frigid. This seemed like the coldest winter I could remember in a long time. When it wasn't freezing out, it was snowing. At least another six inches of snow had fallen overnight. I wondered if the freezing weather came with the invasion. Maybe it would never be warm again.

The hole was covered, so Ozzie carefully brushed a thick layer of it away. "Okay. Here goes nothing."

We all watched as if spellbound as he pushed the camera though the snow, slowly feeding the length of the cord further and further down. He looked at the laptop positioned in front of him, near my feet. I couldn't see what was on the screen, and I wanted to, so I took a step away from the others and began walking toward him.

"No, Zoe." Kyle said.

I stopped. Shot him a look. "I want to see if my sister is down there."

"You will, but just let and Ozzie and I see what's down there first. We don't know what shape the women are in."

Dread crept over me, freezing the blood in my veins. I stepped back.

The others also took a step back. Nobody wanted to see it if it was bad.

"Watch for Zekes," Kyle said.

We lifted our gaze to the woods surrounding us. Once again, I was struck by how stunningly gorgeous it was. This was a scene I would've downloaded from a royalty free photo site to use as background on my laptop. Pure white snow coated the woods and shimmered on the branches of all the trees. The sun filtered through the trees and dappled the snow. It all looked so inviting.

I giggled.

All eyes shifted to me.

"What's so funny?" Ryder asked me, his face quizzical.

"Good day for skiing." I grinned. Then giggled again.

It broke the tension, and everyone chuckled.

"Or snowshoeing," Mina added. "Ever do that?"

I shook my head. "No. Is it fun?"

"I don't know. Never done it," she said.

We all snickered again.

But our gazes kept flicking to Ozzie and Kyle, who were watching the laptop screen intently.

"How about sledding?" Ryder asked. "That hill over there. All you have to do is avoid the trees."

"And the deadies," I said.

"And the holes in the ground," Mina said. "Talk about thrill seeking."

And we all laughed quietly at that. The image in my mind was hysterical for some reason.

Apparently the others thought it was hilarious, too, because they all laughed harder, but without making much sound. Our shoulders shook with the effort of keeping in our laughter.

We kept glancing at Kyle and Ozzie and suddenly we all stopped laughing.

They both stared at the screen, twin looks of abject horror on their faces.

I stepped over to stand behind Ozzie.

"No, Zoe!" Kyle hissed.

But it was too late. I wanted to see what was so awful. I looked at the screen.

The scope camera was apparently hanging about a foot into one of the travel-ways of the crawlers. It lit what looked to be a dug out track where they moved from one area to the other. The tunnel seemed winding and endless, about three feet wide and about as deep from top to bottom. The entire space was covered in a transparent, yellowish, shiny substance.

The bright LED light swung slightly, and cast shadows on the area around it, but it wasn't hard to see the space directly around the camera.

It looked like an underground hive, with holes; pockets dug into the walls, like the cells of a hive.

Inside the pockets were bodies.

They'd been tucked into the cells, and what was visible in the light looked to be jammed unnaturally into the holes. The head of an older man was lying on his feet, his arms stretched outward, fingers poking out of the cell.

Beneath that pocket was a younger man, jammed into the hole sideways. His arms and legs were missing. Only gaping, bloody gouges remained where his legs once were. He squinted up at the light, and blinked. His mouth opened and closed.

Both men were shellacked in a clear, shining substance.

I gagged, turned and fell to my knees, retching in the snow.

NINE

I ran. I ran out into the woods, as far away from the images on Ozzie's laptop screen as I could get. The scene was burned into my mind, and I knew that I'd never, ever be able to erase it from my memory.

The swishing sound of someone's jacket arms moving as they ran after me sounded behind me, beneath the sound of my own choked sobbing.

Finally I stopped at a tree and leaned my arm against it, resting my forehead against the cool, soft material of the ski jacket. Hot tears spilled from my eyes and I couldn't seem to stop crying. I stood there for a long time, not even caring if a deadie got me or not.

I heard somebody breathing behind me, and knew that they were keeping an eye out for the dead.

Slowly, the tears subsided, but I didn't want to uncover my eyes. I didn't want to see any more horrible things. Though continuing to live meant that seeing horrible things was an unavoidable certainty.

This was what living is now.

Sniffling, I lifted my head from my arms and looked behind me.

Ryder stood a few feet back, looking around the woods, then back at me. His eyes were sympathetic and uncertain. "I'm afraid to ask you what you saw."

"Then don't." I took a shuddering breath. "It's horrible."

He dug into his jacket pocket and handed me a tissue. "That one's clean."

I smiled. "You carry tissue in your pocket?"

"Yeah. My mom used to put it in my pocket when I was little. It's just a habit that I picked up as a kid and continued doing. I don't know why. Makes me feel better, in some small way, I guess."

I nodded. "I know what you mean. It's the little things like that. Putting tissue in your pocket or wearing your mother's winter hat," I gestured to my hat. "That make us who we are. We'll all change because of what's happened. But we can keep a tiny part of ourselves. The things that mean something to us. Things that make us human."

He nodded and gave me a uncertain smile. "It'll be okay, Zoe. Right? If we're careful."

I hesitated, then nodded. As much for me as for him. "Yeah."

Kyle was standing beside Ozzie when we walked back, but he stepped in between us and Ozzie as we approached. His face looked sickened. "Don't look at the screen, guys. Okay? Let us gather the data, and then decide what action to take from there. I know it's horrifying, what that camera is picking up down there. But we have to try to remain rational. We have to keep cool heads. You understand?"

Ryder and I both nodded.

"Keep busy. Watch for Zekes. Help keep us safe."

We each gave a single nod and turned our backs from the screen, keeping our eyes on the woods around us.

"And guys," Kyle said.

We turned back to him.

"Watch for holes."

"I COULD'VE FALLEN into one of them running off like that. You could've, and it would've been my fault." I washed a dish and handed it to Ryder. We'd finished eating. Dinner had been spaghetti and salad. We'd skipped lunch to cover as much ground as possible, so we'd all been famished. My belly was full, now, but dinner sat like a stone inside of me.

The hot water on my hands felt good. I was having trouble warming up. The realization that emotions could really kill me was sinking in. Emotions distracted you and made you reckless.

"I was watching." Ryder grinned at me, drying the plate and putting it away in the cupboard.

"But you couldn't have stopped me."

"If I'd yelled I think you would've stopped."

"How many did they find?" There had been several more spray painted trees by the time we'd gone back into the compound.

"I counted five surrounding the building." His face paled as he said this.

A chill moved up my spine. The fear was hard to control. How the hell would I find a way to work through it?

His hand warmed my back, and he looked at me from under dark hair. "I know. It seems impossible, doesn't it? Inevitable that if the deadies don't get us, the crawlers will."

I nodded. My throat tightening. "Yeah."

"I know."

"How are we going to go down there, Ryder? We're all scared shitless. Those things are counting on it. They'll use our fear against us and pick us off like fish in a barrel."

He frowned. "You think they know we're planning to go down there?"

"They know. They're smart. Look at what they've managed to do so far."

"We have to go down there, Zoe. There's a chance the women are still alive. Your sister may be alive down there. My sister. They may all be."

"I can't believe I thought we could all just go down there without knowing what was awaiting us. But then, I kind of wish we hadn't seen it. Now we know what could happen if they get us."

"Forewarned is forearmed."

I stared at the cooling, sudsy water. I was so terrified thinking of what we saw on Ozzie's screen that a pleasant numbness began to spread over me. "It's like, every time I get my courage up, something worse happens and I think we're all going to die, and then I wonder if it matters to even try."

Hank nudged me in the leg with his head. He'd been lying on the kitchen floor, and was sensitive to the tone of my voice and my body language. I patted his head and he rubbed the top of his nose into my hand.

"Well, Hank is still up for fighting. If he can do it, so can we." Ryder bent down and stroked Hank's back.

I managed a small laugh.

We had no choice. We'd go down into the ground and find the loved ones that had been snatched from us, and get them out of there. And if we failed, we'd go down fighting, not cowering.

Only now we had another long night ahead of us, knowing what was waiting for us when we did venture down into the ground.

WE TOOK turns keeping watch again. When my turn came, Ryder sat up with me. Having him beside me helped to keep the fear just a notch down from paralyzing.

There were more of them now. The sounds of clawing, scratching, thudding and thumping were everywhere. They were covering more of the compound. I could picture them, crawling all around, their reptilian, greenish grey bodies, dome-like heads and insect-like arms and legs.

I squeezed my eyes shut, trying to will the images away.

Huddled close together, we listened to the nightmare outside until dawn.

AT FIRST LIGHT we headed toward the woods. I crouched and kissed Hank on the head. "Take care of things here, buddy. Okay? I'll see you soon."

He didn't look happy about it, but he didn't complain.

As we stood around a hole my entire body trembled. I gripped a handheld UV light in one hand. I moved my hand over the belt tied around my waist to make sure the screwdriver was still tucked into it. I'd already checked several times, but I couldn't seem to stop myself checking again.

Thick, fat snowflakes floated down on chilled wind, and we were all looking grim as we watched Ozzie and Kyle get ready for our first expedition into hell.

"I'll go down first," Ozzie said. "The holes have a steep

but definite angle to them. They don't go straight downward. They slope for a few yards, then even out. They're like underground caves. So if we're careful, nobody will get hurt going down. We can't afford to have our focus on anything but what's in that hole. Got it?"

We all nodded.

"Okay," Kyle said. "Ozzie, then me, then Zoe, then Ryder, Mina, then Wilson. Okay?"

I understood. If Wilson was going to turn tail and run, he'd have a clear path out, instead of knocking anyone down and trampling over them to get away.

"Got it," Ryder said.

Everyone followed suit.

"Okay. Here goes." Ozzie lowered himself into the hole, slowly crawling backwards on hands and knees. He wore a hard hat with a light on it. We all did, courtesy of Ozzie's plumbing and sewer business. It kept our hands free for weapons and UV lights.

My nerves jangled, and the fight or flight instinct made my heart thump crazily in my chest. My breaths came in little pants, and although it was cold out, my back felt slick with sweat.

I didn't think any of us would make it out of that hole.

But we couldn't live with ourselves if we didn't try.

I glanced up at Wilson, whose eyes were huge with fear. The hand holding his UV light shook visibly and he kept taking a step back, realizing it, and stepping forward again.

Although he'd saved my life when the deadie had fallen on top of me, I didn't trust him. He made me nervous. I looked up at Ryder, whose eyes were also shifting from the hole to Wilson.

When Ozzie's hard hat vanished into the hole, Kyle

positioned himself on his hands and knees and began crawling down into the depths.

"You okay, Oz?" he asked.

"Right as rain," Ozzie's slightly echoed voice floated up.

We all snickered nervously. It couldn't be less right, going down into the ground, serving ourselves up as snacks to those things.

Our smiles vanished as Kyle's hard hat disappeared into the hole.

"You're up," Ryder said, patting the back of my ski jacket. "I'll be right behind you."

I turned and got down on my hands and knees as Ozzie and Kyle had, and slowly began moving backwards, down into the depths.

The light from my hard hat threw eerie shadows around me, and the smell was sickly sweet and strange. Shiny, yellowish brown goo coated the ground all around me, and I had the horrifying sensation of being swallowed by some strange, giant creature.

"Go easy, Zoe." Kyle's voice was close. He was only a few feet down from me. "Things level off here, but the nightmare begins. Okay?"

I nodded, so afraid I could barely think, but then realized that he couldn't see me nodding. "Okay."

Moving slowly and carefully, I followed Kyle deeper into the tunnel. My skin crawled beneath my clothes, and sweat beaded my chest and back. Fear screamed at me to scramble back up and out of the cave, but I fought against it.

My sister was down here, somewhere.

Ryder moved above me, moving slowly downward, and then I heard Mina. They were shapes against the bright shine of the UV light. I was too far down to see daylight above me anymore. I may never see it again.

We kept moving downward.

A shout from above, a startled scream.

Wilson.

Kyle used his walkie-talkie. "What's going on?"

Mina responded. "Wilson slipped. It freaked him out. He's a little jumpy, but he's okay."

"He's gonna give me a damned heart attack!" Kyle said.

I heard Ozzie swear below me. Another reason for him to dislike Wilson. He might just get us all killed.

I heard Kyle's quick, terrified gasps, and the horrified curses under his breath.

A moment later the cells in the hive-like walls were on either side of me.

I didn't want to look. What I'd seen on Ozzie's laptop screen was so horrific, I never wanted to see it again. But having it come alive all around me was blood-curdling.

I kept telling myself I was dreaming. I'd wake up in my own bed, and it would be Sunday morning. I'd make pancakes for me and Jessica and let Kelly and Derek sleep in. We'd watch cartoons together, bundled up on the couch with a blanket...

I heard a sound from my left. Instinct made me turn to look.

My light fell on the face of a man, still wearing his thick framed Buddy Holly glasses. He stared at me, his eyes wide with abject terror. His mouth was working, but only moans coming out.

Only the top half of him remained, one arm missing. The button-down shirt he wore on the day he was snatched stuck to his skin. What was left of him was covered in the shiny, transparent yellowy substance.

"Oh, my God." I sobbed into the back of my ski glove.

Kyle came up close. "Don't stop, Zoe."

"But he's trying to tell us something. We can't just ignore him."

Kyle hesitated, crawled up beside me and looked at the man, his face betraying the sympathy he felt for him.

The man continued trying to talk, making guttural, liquid noises deep in his throat. He began coughing and gagging.

Kyle began to move backward again. "I can't. I can't."

Again, the man's mouth moved, forming silent words.

"Wait!" I whispered. "He's trying to say something again. He might know where the women are, Kyle."

Kyle hesitated, and then moved back upward again. He watched as the man's fingers moved. His arm was jammed underneath him, but he managed to move his fingers in a 'come closer' gesture.

Kyle leaned in, watched the man's face closely.

"Paw-ket," the man's voice was barely audible. "Paw-ket."

"Pocket," I said. "Look in his pocket."

Kyle slowly moved his hand toward the man's shirt pocket. It was flattened with sticky substance. "Here?"

The man nodded his head as best he could.

Kyle worked his fingers into the pocket, causing a ripping sound as the dried substance gave and the top of the pocket opened. He pulled out a flash drive.

The man blinked a 'yes.' Then mouthed, "G-Go," over and over.

His eyes fluttered and closed.

I cried, silently, my nose running, tears spilling from my eyes. My chest hitched and constricted and I suddenly could barely breathe.

This was too much. Humans weren't meant to see such terrible things.

If the crawlers woke up, we'd be dragged down into the depths, partially eaten, and coated in that shiny substance. We'd be tucked away in cells of our own, every one of us. Until they came back to feed again.

Maybe except me and Mina. Maybe they'd have a special place for us.

An unbearable urge washed over me. I wanted to scream and scream until I had no voice left.

Then someone did.

"ZEKES!" Wilson screamed from above us and, then screamed again, the sound high and shrill.

My heart slammed in my ribcage. How many?

He screamed like he was being torn apart.

The voice of Ryder above me, "Go down! Go! There are a bunch of them!"

Wilson had been the last in the hole. The deadies must've seen him or heard him yell when he slipped.

"Down!" Mina screamed. "Go!"

We couldn't fight them. Not down here.

Gunshots. Mina and Ryder were firing.

Kyle scrambled past me. "Zoe, go find another hole! We need to get out."

I lost my foothold and slid downward. I was being swallowed by the cave, like I was in the esophagus sliding toward the depths of the belly.

Find a hole to escape out of.

I kept chanting this in my mind, moving backward, my hands and feet gripping the yellowed, hardened ground.

The hive flanked both sides of me. I looked into cells and I moved downward, trying to find Kelly, but the people shoved into the holes were older women, men, and boys in their teens.

I looked up as I descended, searching for an escape opening.

More shouts up from above.

Ryder was suddenly at my side, and Mina was directly above me.

I moved quickly, the partially eaten people on both sides of me pleading with their eyes, mouths opening and closing, or screaming silently.

Wanting to shut my eyes against the gruesome, horrific scene around me, I looked down at the tunnel below me, frantically looking for an escape route.

Finally the tunnel leveled out and I stopped moving downward, and suddenly there were several trails to take. Without thinking I took the right.

I crawled, my knees becoming raw beneath my jeans.

There was light ahead.

I was all but throwing myself forward now, my arms and legs burning with the effort. The strange, sweet smell of the substance was cloying in my nostrils.

And then there it was. An opening, only feet ahead of us.

I crawled and threw myself toward the filtered light in the ceiling of the tunnel. My lungs strained for breath. I felt as if I was suffocating.

The walls around me seemed to be turning. I was becoming disoriented.

I was going to die down here.

With a shove from Ryder behind me, it was directly above us.

Ryder pushed me up, shoving me toward the exit, higher and higher.

And then I was climbing up onto the frozen, white ground, the snow falling onto my face.

Ryder came up next, only a moment after I hit the surface.

Next came Mina.

Ozzie.

Kyle.

Wilson didn't make it out.

We were running, then. Running toward the compound as the snow fell harder, coming down sideways, driven by a raging wind.

"THE ZEKES HEARD WILSON. Must've been wandering near the compound." Ozzie paced the floor, agitated. "Damn it!"

Kyle built a fire, and we sat around it, needing its heat. The cold of the underground tunnels had seeped deep into our bones.

I looked up at Kyle, who squatted near the fire, eyes lost in the flames. His face creased with worry. "What's on the flash drive?"

He looked at me, his face momentarily blank. "I forgot about that, Zoe."

"What flash drive?" Ozzie asked.

Kyle dug the little blue flash drive from his coat pocket. "One of the people in the hive. A man. He managed to tell me to look in his pocket. In it was this flash drive."

"Well, let's see what's on it." Ozzie held out his hand and Kyle dropped the flash drive into his palm.

Ozzie put the little flash drive into a USB port on his laptop, which rested on the kitchen table.

I looked over at Sherry. "How is Logan doing?"

She gave a weak smile. "He's doing better. His fever is gone. His wounds are healing, amazingly."

"Thanks to you," I said. "I'll go in and see him in a minute."

"I think he'd like that. He was awake a little while ago."

"This guy was an anthropologist," Ozzie said, reading a document he brought up from on the flash drive. "Jason Barrows. Doctor of Anthropology with the Lawrence Institute in Albany. He was some kind of researcher."

We gathered around the table, looking at Ozzie's screen.

"Dr. Barrows was watching these things for quite a spell, it seems. He first came upon them on a dig up in the Adirondacks. Apparently he found the first hole a month ago."

"Good of him to let the rest of the world know that we were about to be invaded," Mina said. "Strong work."

"He went down there twice," Ozzie said. "There's no mention of people being stowed in holes in the walls. But he does mention a hive-like structure. Listen, 'It would appear that the hive-live structure may be for sleeping or hibernating purposes. The underground tunnels are both insect-like and cave-like in design. The bones I found yesterday on my dig are like the ones I found in Greece last autumn."

These creatures are prehistoric, and insect-like in formation but not in composition. These are definitely bones. They appear to be of the Pleistocene era. They would've thrived in a glacial atmosphere. More bones were laid out nearby. The proximity of the bones to others suggests an ancient burial ground the creatures used. The underground trails and tunnels I've discovered are fresh. These creatures had to have found a way to thrive in warmer conditions their ancestors wouldn't have tolerated. It seems they've evolved. They've made a comeback.'"

"They lived during the Ice Age." Ryder straightened, looking at me. "But they're back? What happened? When their food died off, they died off?"

"Maybe," Kyle said.

"Wait," Ozzie continued reading. "He says they may have continued to survive in glacial areas."

"Like the arctic?" Sherry squinted at the screen.

"Maybe," Kyle said.

"So these things hadn't eaten or stored anyone at the time Dr. Barrows wrote this," Mina said.

"No," I said. "They were preparing for it. Getting their storage area ready."

"There's a link here," Ozzie said. He clicked the hyperlink and a slideshow appeared on the screen. Ozzie clicked the option to manually operate the slideshow.

The first photo was of the bones Dr. Jason Barrows had discovered on his dig in Greece. They were freakish and strange, and knowing what we knew now, absolutely terrifying.

The bones were laid out on a white table. They were insect-like. I counted four legs on either side of the body. The head was elongated, the face turned toward the camera. The mouth was open to expose three rows of razor sharp teeth."

"Oh, my God," Mina said.

"Those don't look like the ones we've seen," Ozzie said.

"Let's look at the other pictures," Kyle said.

Ozzie clicked to another shot. More bones, the same as the last photo, but laid out on its back. The under belly of the thing was covered in rings, similar to ribs, but without the space in the middle. "This shit is out of a horror movie."

There were nine more photos of the bones from the dig in Greece, then photos of the bones he'd found in the Adirondacks. There were two of the creatures, bones exactly the same in structure. The older bones were the same insect-like structure as the newer bones. Similar creatures, but changed.

"There are similarities, but there's no guarantee that these are the same things that we're dealing with now," Sherry said.

"We may never know," I said. "Dr. Barrows is stuffed in one of their underground hives."

"No one else knew about this?" Sherry said.

"This guy thought he had the find of the century," Ryder said. "He didn't tell anyone."

"Yeah," Ozzie said. "He was thinking book deals, TV, and movie rights. He didn't want to share. He wanted to keep his little discovery all to himself."

Mina snorted. "Well, that was a bad call."

"Yeah. He did have the find of the century," I said. "Just before they started eating us."

TEN

Another night passed, but the scratching sounds were muted by the storm outside. The wind howled; snow thunder split through the night. I'd only ever heard thunder during a snow storm once before, when I was little, and at the time I thought it was the coolest thing ever. Now it just made me jittery. I didn't know what was worse, being able to hear the crawlers scratching and thumping against the windows and roof, or not being able to hear them.

I wanted to look in on Logan, but knowing that these things sense movement, I didn't dare. Sherry slept on the cot next to him, so at least he wasn't alone.

Earlier, before the dark came, I went in to see him. He lay still on the bed, eyes droopy from the pain killer Sherry had given him. He lifted his hand slightly from the comforter, indicating that he wanted me to come and see him.

The sharp smell of antiseptic only barely covered the sick smell coming off of him. Although his fever had broken, the sweetish stench of it still clung to him, despite Sherry sponging him off earlier.

"I think I might live," he croaked. "But I don't know if I'm happy about that or not."

"I know." I patted his hand and sat on the bed next to him. "But you are one tough S.O.B. So you might as well just get better and not fight it."

He smiled weakly. "I thought I was dead."

"We all thought we were going to die when that horde came through the door." I was struck by how gaunt and haunted he looked. He could easily be mistaken for one of the dead.

"What happened earlier? Sherry won't tell me anything, and it's worse not knowing. Being left with my imagination."

I doubted that. But I told him anyway. "We went underground earlier. It went bad. Lost Wilson. He slipped. Shouted. A bunch of deadies followed him in the hole."

"Damn. I'm sorry to hear it. He seemed like an okay guy."

"Yeah."

"Did you see any crawlers?" His voice was hesitant, like he wasn't sure he wanted to know.

I shook my head. I wasn't about to tell him about the half eaten people stored in the holes of the underground hive. It was definitely a tidbit he didn't need to know about. It could still happen to him --- to any of us.

He was getting better. But it would be a while before he could fight against deadies or crawlers.

"Nope. I think we were driven out of that tunnel too soon."

"Probably a good thing."

I nodded and gave him a smile.

The absence of sound startled me back to the here and now. The wind had died down, and all was silent. Mina was on watch, and as I looked over at her, her gaze locked with mine.

"It's daylight," she said, but she didn't look relieved.

We were going back underground today.

THE SNOW FELL thick and fast. It seemed like winter would never end as we made our way out to the woods. Snowflakes fell on my cheeks and lashes, and down the back of my neck. I wanted to put my hood on, but the hood would obscure my peripheral vision. It occurred to me that if I lay down on the ground right then I'd be completely covered in no time.

Which reminded me to keep a lookout for holes.

Judging from the hunched shoulders of everyone around me, we all were dreading the second promenade into the underground tunnels.

Ozzie and Kyle decided that we'd try a different hole this time, in hopes of finding one closer to where the women were being kept. They chose a hole on the opposite side of compound, about a quarter of a mile away.

He stopped at the hole next to a large oak spray painted with a red "X", then turned to the group. "Everyone keep watch. We don't need any surprises coming through the snow at us."

It was also his way of making sure we didn't see what was on the screen quite yet. He didn't want us going down there blind, but he didn't want to prolong the dread we felt before going in, either.

We all kept our eyes to the woods around us. The snow was falling so quickly now that it was hard to see within a ten foot distance. But we squinted against the snow and peered into the woods, doing slow turns every few seconds.

"Zeke." Ryder pointed to an area somewhere to the left. "Slow mover."

It was a man wearing an orange jumpsuit. He slowly trudged along the snow, arms barely moving at his sides. He spotted us, and he began his slack-jawed journey our way.

"That's prison wear," Mina said. "He must've escaped while being transferred or something."

"Anything and everything could've happened when the shit first began to fly," Ozzie said. "Birchwood Prison isn't far from here."

Kyle nodded over toward the deadie. "The cold might be making them slower, which is good, but it might make us reckless, too. Go on and get him. Use your knife. We don't need bullets drawing more of them."

"Yeah," Ozzie said, drilling a hole into the frozen ground. "Let's not have a repeat of yesterday."

"You don't think the sound of the drill will draw them?" I asked.

"I'm already done. And the drill isn't that loud. We need to see what we're heading into." He laid the drill aside and began feeding the camera and cord down into the ground, watching the screen with furrowed brows.

I watched Ryder as he approached the deadie. The deadie made grunting noises and it stiffly walked toward him. He raised his arms and his hands opened and closed as he shambled over the drifts.

When the deadie was only about a foot from him, Ryder plunged his knife into the deadie's eye, then stepped back, pulling the knife out as the deadie dropped. He wiped the blade off in the snow, leaving gore streaks on pure white.

Ryder's face was devoid of expression as he made his

way back. He's already killed enough deadies to be unaffected by it. I wondered if I had, too.

Just last week we all had lives. Maybe not great lives, but they had to be a hell of a lot better than the life we were living now. If you could call it living.

Ozzie made a choking sound, and I swung my head around to look at him.

The back of his hand was jammed against his mouth, his face contorted into a mask of pain. He'd fallen back into the snow, and small, silent sobs hitched in the back of his throat.

Kyle had fallen to his knees, the heels of both gloved hands covering his eyes. He whispered, "Oh, God. Oh, God. Oh, no. No. No. No."

We all stood frozen, staring at them.

My legs began trembling, and then tremors moved up my entire body. I broke out in a cold sweat, and my scalp crawled. I breathed, "What is it?"

Ozzie's petrified gaze shot up to mine, and he shook his head. "I can't . . . I can't fathom it."

Kyle rocked back and forth, his shoulders shaking, still whispering, "No, no, no, no."

Ryder, Mina and I looked at each other, fear and dread were plain on their faces.

With my heart drilling in my chest, I stepped over to Ozzie, crouching beside him. I placed a hand on his arm, and slowly turned toward the screen.

My heart stopped.

It was more horrible than my worst imaginings.

The scope camera had been dropped through the ceiling of a breeding room.

Rows of women hung by their feet, naked in yellowish, transparent, cocoon-like sacks, their eyes wide open, mouths yawning in silent screams. Blood spilled over their shellacked foreheads and puddled onto the ground beneath their heads. The yellow substance around their mouths had been burst through. Holes marred the perfect varnish of the cocoon that had covered them. Something had crawled out of their mouths. Something that had been inside of them.

Suddenly I couldn't get enough oxygen into my lungs. I fell away from the screen, gulping at the air, making whimpering sounds deep in my throat.

Then my entire being rejected what I'd seen, and I emptied my belly onto the snow.

WE STOOD around the hole looking at each other, like we could find strength from the others, if just one of us found a way to pull it together. Every one of us was trying to catch our breath. We'd all expected to see something bad on Ozzie's screen, but not one of us was prepared for the horror only a few feet below us.

Finally, Kyle was able to form words. He leaned over, hands on his thighs, looking up at us. "Did any of you recognize any of those women?"

We all shook our heads.

He straightened, with effort. His strength had gone out of him, but he was fighting to get it back. "Then there is a chance that our loved ones are still alive."

We nodded, still stunned, but I don't think any of us believed that to be true. We hung on to Kyle's fine, precarious thread of hope because it was all that we could do.

I looked at Mina and found her wild, dark gaze penetrating mine, and I knew what she was thinking.

What if we were caught? What if Kyle, Ozzie and Ryder were stowed in the hive as food, and we were caught?

We'd be strung up and bagged, and implanted with alien eggs, or however else they impregnated their prey, just like all the other women. We'd hang there, upside down in a dark cave, waiting until the monster inside of us slithered up through our throats and out of our mouths, killing us in the process.

Dead people don't bleed. Those women were alive when those things crawled out of them.

I swallowed, and tried to slow my panicked heart.

Ozzie took a few breaths, walked a slow circle, looking up at the sky, then turned to us. "These poor women were likely some of the first to be grabbed. Kelly, Melody, Cassie, Marnie, Diane, and Penny may be in another room somewhere. But we need to be prepared for the very real possibility . . . likelihood, that they've been impregnated."

No one said a word. We let his statement sink in.

Ozzie wiped the back of a glove over his mouth, then lifted his hand. His voice had lost most of the conviction he'd shown before. "We get in. We find them. We get them out. We deal with everything else afterward. Okay?"

"Yeah," I said. The word stuck in my throat like a bone.

"Okay," Ryder said, forcing more courage into his tone than he felt.

"Got it. Let's just get them out." Mina placed her hands on her hips. Her face had hardened, but her lips quivered slightly.

We were all scared shitless.

I felt my stomach clench at the idea of going down into the tunnels again. It seemed that each discovery we made was worse than the last.

"Okay, are we ready?" Ozzie asked, his gaze shifting to each one of us.

Everyone answered in the affirmative.

Ozzie gave a single nod. "I'll go down first, then Zoe, Ryder, Mina, and then Kyle."

"Who is going to watch for Zekes?" Ryder asked. "It could happen again."

"I am."

We all turned in the direction of the voice.

Sherry approached us in a snow white parka, a white, fuzzy hat on her head. "I'm not letting you guys go down there without a look-out, and you need every one of you to back each other up."

"Logan okay to stay alone for a bit?" Kyle asked her.

"Yeah. He's safe where he is."

No one stated the obvious, which was that if we all died underground and Sherry was overcome by deadies, Logan would likely die.

But then, we might lose us all if we were overcome by deadies again while we were underground.

Six of one, half dozen of the other.

We didn't have a lot of options.

"Thanks, Sherry," I said.

"Of course," she said. "Now get going. Get our ladies back."

Ozzie flicked on the light on his hard hat and lowered himself down into the hole, his handheld UV light clipped to his belt. He paused. "As soon as the ground levels out, everyone get your UV light in hand. Understood?"

We all nodded.

Numbness spread over me as fear clawed at my stomach. Dread filled my chest and made it hard to breathe. I forced my legs to move toward the hole as Ozzie disappeared into the darkness, the light on his hard hat bouncing around the entrance to the tunnel.

My movements felt stiff as I tried to get a grip on my panic. The roaring in my ears made it harder to coordinate myself enough not to lose my grip and go sliding into Ozzie. The knowledge that we were heading into a very real hell made me look up at the sky above us, certain that this would be the very last time that I'd ever see the light of day again.

And worse, the possibility; the likelihood that Mina and I could be trussed up and hung like the other females underground made death the more desirable of the two evils.

Stop! Just stop! You have a job to do. A mission to complete. Do it.

I followed Ozzie down further into the underground. The hardened varnish-like, yellow substance was everywhere, keeping the dirt from caving in.

At least there's that.

A powerful urge to laugh hysterically came over me, and I shoved it down. Now wasn't the time to lose it.

Oh, now is the time to lose it. If those things get us, you don't want to be lucid. No, not at all.

Still, I fought the urge and continued moving downward. Every hand-hold, foot-hold, that led me further into the cave brought with it a new level of dread and terror. I wished I was back at the college picking cheerleader gum off my mop. Those were the good old days.

Those girls were almost certainly down here somewhere. I didn't want to see them.

I didn't want to see any of them.

"Okay, Zoe." Ozzie's voice shook. "Here's where it levels off. The room where the girls are is behind me."

I heard Ozzie's deep intake of breath, preparing for the sight we saw on his laptop screen.

Another couple of steps downward and the tunnel leveled off, just like he said.

With my nerves jangling beneath my skin, I turned. I looked up and around me. There were no holes in the walls in this part of the tunnel. No hive.

But the sickly sweet smell, with the tang of pennies beneath it made my stomach roil.

Ozzie stood a couple of yards away, just inside the opening of the cave-like space used for breeding. His face was a sickly green, and I was sure it wasn't entirely because of the color of the shiny walls around him being reflected back in the light of his hard hat. He stared at me, his face pained. He didn't want to turn around.

But he did. Slowly.

A shuddering breath came out of him then, and a thin, forlorn whimper.

"Ozzie, we have to do this." I couldn't believe I had the courage to say this to him. I was beyond afraid; beyond terror. But somehow I found the strength to keep functioning through it. "Think of our girls."

He nodded, leaning over and looking around at each face through the filmy, gossamer sacks, not unlike gluey spider webbing.

I did the same, following him.

The abject horror and pain of what had happened to them was frozen on their faces in death. Shock stamped in their wide eyes forever.

Even as it was happening, they simply hadn't been able to believe it.

Mina came up behind us, then Ryder and Kyle. Sounds of mortification came from them all.

Face after face, I looked for Kelly, following Ozzie's hitched breathing and shadowed figure.

Mina, Ryder, and Kyle did the same.

There had to be twenty women in the room.

"What about Logan's sister?" I whispered.

"I saw a pic of her on his phone. She's not here." Mina's voice cracked.

Ozzie turned toward us, taking several breaths and pressing the back of his hand over his nose. The smell of blood was sharp in this room. Stepping in it was unavoidable. He closed his eyes for a moment before speaking. "Let's keep going. There have to be other rooms like this down here."

We followed him out of the room, all of us moving slowly, our UV lights in hand.

The tunnel broke apart into four separate trails.

"Maybe we should separate," Mina said. "We could cover more ground that way."

"No," Ozzie said. "We stay together. Those things could be anywhere." He stopped, looked down a corridor to our right, lowering his head a little to shine his light through the tunnel. The light revealed a row of openings on either side of the underground trail.

He stood in front of the other trails, shining his light in each.

Each corridor had rows of openings, and separate, smaller caves.

"Good, Christ," he murmured. "Help us."

WE MOVED FORWARD, slowly, and I thought I could hear everyone's heart beating in my ears. My legs felt leaden as I forced myself to take another step toward the horror that awaited us. And another. All of my senses sharpened. I heard every breath, every scrape against the strange shellacked floor of the cave. I saw each shape within my sights more clearly. The smell of rotting meat and blood assaulted my nostrils and made me gag.

It was so cold. Every breath seemed to freeze my lungs a little more.

My entire body trembled, and if I allowed myself to think about what I'd see, I'd lose it.

So I just kept moving.

Ozzie moved into the first opening in the walls, his UV light lifted, ready.

The scene in this cave was like the last. We searched each terror-stricken, tortured face, all of us swiping away tears. It was too horrible.

We couldn't harden ourselves to it. We had no defenses against it.

We continued, cave after cave.

And then a cry rang out. And another. And another. Then screams.

We all froze.

The hair lifted on my scalp and my heart leapt into my throat.

Then we were moving. We ran in the direction of the screams.

They grew louder and shriller with every opening we passed, every cave housing roomfuls of hanging women, until finally we reached them.

A cave with women whose cocoons hadn't been torn outward. Not yet.

We ran in, looking at faces.

"Oh, God. They're moving. Their bellies are moving," Ryder cried.

I looked down at the belly of the woman hanging in front of me. Her stomach was undulating.

And she was shrieking, her fingers clawing at the skin of her belly.

I took a step back, banging into another hanging, screaming woman.

We all stumbled back.

Except Ozzie, who dropped to his knees and wailed, his hands on the belly of the woman hanging in front of him. "Noooo! Noooo! NOOOOO! NOOOOOO!"

Kyle stared, wide-eyed for a moment, then blinked and ran forward, grabbing Ozzie under the arms and hauling him back.

"Let go of me! It's Diane! It's Diane!" Ozzie yelled.

"Something is coming out of her, Ozzie. We need to stay back." Kyle yanked him backward. "UV lights! UV lights!"

When the first of the creatures moved upward, a strange, snake-like shape moving beneath the skin of Diane's chest, up into her neck, her screams were cut off. The thing tore through her throat as Diane's body convulsed. A greenish grey thing poked it's head out through her stretched lips and screeched at us, rows of tiny serrated teeth snapping.

Mina stepped forward, aiming the UV light straight at the creature.

Dark, glistening, spindly arms emerged from the mouth, smoking in the UV light. The small, dome-like head shook back and forth, and then the thing let out a high pitched shriek as the head fell into itself and disintegrated into a smoky, slimy substance hanging from her mouth.

Ryder did the same with the woman hanging to her right.

But there were too many of them.

We stepped further back, toward the opening and aimed our UV lights at the things as they burst from their screaming, choking mothers and scrambled like insects away from us, skittering up the walls and over the ceiling of the cave, hissing and screeching.

They burned, sizzled and disintegrated, the gooey remains plopping to the cave floor.

Then it was quiet, except for our frantic gasping and Ozzie's helpless sobbing.

Kyle looked up and frowned. He lifted his hand. "Shhh."

We all held our breath, listening.

A low hissing sound came from down the corridor.

"Move! Those things are coming!"

We ran into the corridor, but when we came to the area where the tunnels branched off, we stopped.

"Which way?" Ozzie asked.

"Left!" Kyle shouted.

We moved as fast as we could in the close confines of the tunnel, ducking down as the hissing grew louder.

And then Mina screamed.

And then Ryder screamed.

They were everywhere, skittering along the walls and the ceilings.

I lifted my UV light and aimed for the ceiling, still moving forward, blinded by Ozzie and Kyle's lights.

A crawler directly above me sizzled and screeched, and fell behind me, and I kept aiming and moving.

Things moving along the walls crackled and shrieked,

the steam and smoke coming from them burning my nostrils and eyes, and I couldn't see any longer.

I swung my UV light crazily, waiting to be grabbed by the claws of a crawler directly behind me. It was so close I could feel its stinking breath on my neck. I rolled, light held up, and heard the thing fall backwards, bursting like fireworks. Scrambling backwards, I kept moving upward, heading toward the entrance, toward the daylight, sure that another was coming up on me.

My throat burned as I burst through to the surface, scrambling up onto the snow. I continued aiming my UV light into the hole, hoping to get as many crawlers as I could, willing whoever was left to make it back up to the light.

Snow fell fast on my face and I opened my eyes to stinging slits, trying to see enough to make my aim true.

With blurred vision, my eyes burning, I saw Kyle burst through into the falling snow, then Ozzie coming up behind him. His arms reached the surface as he pulled and crawled toward us. Both hands reached the snow, his eyes round with terror.

And then two ovaloid, smoking heads appeared in the murky light and his mouth opened in a scream as they pulled him back into the depths.

ELEVEN

Sherry lifted me under the arms and dragged me toward the compound. "Run! I hear the dead coming!"

Through bleary, raw eyes I squinted into the storm, but couldn't see more than a few feet in front of us. "Where? Where are they? I can't see!"

We were running through a white-out blizzard. Stumbling, our arms in front of us, trying to feel our way around. *This is what being snow blind is.* The blizzard couldn't have come at a worse time.

I felt a hand grab my arm and breath on my ear, and my heart froze.

Kyle said, low. "Move slowly and carefully. Stay close to me."

Sherry moved beside me, staying close to Kyle as he led the way. We were silent, not even the sound of our labored breathing could be heard as we walked blindly through the blizzard.

The howling of the wind confused our ears. It was hard to tell the difference between what we'd come to know as the groans of a deadie and the moaning of the wind.

Spitting snow whipped into my eyes, soothing them of the stinging, but obscuring my vision further. I grasped for Kyle's jacket, but came up with nothing.

Bringing my hands up to my eyes I tried to rub the icy water from the snow out of them.

When I opened them again, Kyle and Sherry had vanished.

I was alone again, with the dead searching for something to eat in the storm.

Logan was alone with no one to help him.

Hank was waiting for me in the compound. If Logan died and Sherry and Kyle didn't make it back, and I froze to death or was caught by a deadie, he'd starve.

And then I was sobbing silently, tears spilling from my eyes and freezing on my face.

I couldn't stand the thought of Hank being alone, waiting for me and dying a sad and lonely death.

A white hot rage came up from my belly and warmed me, and then I felt completely pissed off. I was seventeen years old, damn it. And I'd been through more hell in the past few days than most people in horror films had to endure.

This was bullshit.

I was making it back to that compound, back to my dog.

I blinked the tears away, and was surprised to find that my eyes felt better, and I could even see.

Lifting my arms out in front of me, I continued walking. Slowly, carefully walking.

It seemed I walked for a long time, the cold wrapping around me like a heavy, frozen blanket.

And then I was on my knees. I didn't even remember falling. I stayed like that for a while, my eyes growing so heavy. If I rested just for a minute. . .

A moaning sound, turning into snarling. A figure emerged from the swirling white, walking slow and stiff.

I tried to grab my knife from my boot. I couldn't feel my fingers. I got it, lifted it out, and then dropped it in the snow.

Plunging my hands into the snow I felt around for it. I came up with it grasped in both hands. I waited until the deadie fell onto his knees in front of me to take a bite, and then summoned all the strength I had and used both hands to thrust my knife into his eye.

Using my entire body, I yanked my knife out, then pushed myself to my feet and kept moving.

Another figure emerged from the white.

A big, bounding body with a blocky head.

"Hank!" My voice was lost in the wind, but he heard me.

He jumped toward me, and seemed to smile at me through the snow, and I grabbed onto his collar.

"Take me home, Hank. Back to the compound. I can't see where I'm going, buddy."

And he did.

WHEN THE STORM SLOWED, I took a short walk to the edge of the woods to look for Sherry and Kyle. The storm had receded to a fine dusting. Fine powder floated in the air around us as we stepped out into the winter wonderland of nightmares.

I saw my own tracks, under a layer of fresh fallen snow. It hadn't taken long for Hank to lead me back to the compound. I'd been wandering in circles only a little ways from the fence.

Peering through the white I scanned the area for any

sign of Sherry and Kyle, I had to accept what I already knew. There were none.

Hank stayed close to me as I headed toward the fence. He whined, then barked, and sniffed at the ground.

I stopped and watched as he carefully nudged a spot on the snow. He whimpered, tapped at the ground and then took a few steps back, letting out another sharp bark.

My pulse throbbed in my throat as I looked at the area he'd pawed at, trepidation clenching in my chest. I crouched, using a broken twig lying near me to clear snow from the area.

He whimpered again, and then let out a low snarl.

The edge of the hole emerged as I continued to clear snow from it.

I stood up and stepped back, my body humming with fear. Scanning the ground, I noticed several slightly dented areas dotting the edge of the woods. There were so many more than before, only a few yards apart from each other.

This was how they trapped their food.

If it hadn't been for Hank, I would've likely gone under. I would've fallen into this hole, just like Wilson's father had.

Kyle and Sherry had dropped through holes in the storm. I was sure of it. There were no bloody remains in the snow or deadies tearing into anyone. In fact, there were no deadies at all right now.

Maybe they had all fallen through, too. What did they do with the deadies? Did they eat them?

How close had I come from falling into a hole earlier, wandering, snowblind in the storm? Had I been that lucky? Or had the new holes just not appeared yet?

Industrious bastards.

"Come on, boy. Careful of the holes." I'd said the word

so many times since the invasion had begun, Hank knew what it meant.

We both watched the ground carefully as we made it back to the compound.

Logan had been sleeping when Hank and I burst through the door of the compound earlier. He had still been sleeping when I checked on him before going back to look for Kyle and Sherry.

It was deathly quiet in the compound, as Hank followed me to Logan's room. A creeping sense of dread slithered up my spine and I felt my skin rise into gooseflesh. As we came closer to the room, I noted that Logan's steady, quiet snoring was absent.

Maybe he's awake.

I stopped outside the door and looked down at Hank. His hackles were up, and his head was lowered as he let out a growl, deep in his throat.

My chest tightened and fear buzzed through me.

Oh Christ, he's dead. He's dead.

As if in response to my thought, a strange inhuman groan sounded from the bedroom.

I grabbed the screwdriver from my belt and waited.

"Logan." My hand shook.

Hank let out a growling bark.

Logan growled, too, the sound urgent and hungry.

My heartbeat hammered in my ears as I waited.

Logan shuffled out of the bedroom, his hair matted to his head, his eyes milky grey. His mouth opened and his lips stretched over his teeth.

Raising the screwdriver, I waited until he came a little closer.

When he was a couple of feet from me I stepped forward and shoved the screwdriver through his ear.

His mouth opened wide and he crumpled to the ground.

Sadness welled up inside of me and I backed away, a sob escaping my throat. Tears filled my eyes, and my throat constricted.

I was alone. I was the last human left alive at the compound.

In the entire world, for all I knew.

All I had left was Hank.

Dropping the screwdriver, I sank to the floor, covering my face with my hands. Hank licked my hands and I wrapped my arms around him and buried my face in his neck, my breaths hitching and I let loose and cried into his fur.

I stayed like that for a long time, until I had run out of tears to cry.

Then I wiped my face with my forearm and took a deep, shuddering breath. "Gotta get a grip, huh, boy."

Hank followed me outside as I searched the ground for new holes. The area back to the compound looked free of dents, but I knew there had to be holes out there. Hank and I were careful as we walked back.

"We can't stay here, boy." The crawlers knew I was here. It would be only a matter of maybe another day before the area around the compound was so full of holes that there wouldn't be anywhere for Hank and me to go. They'd get us.

I didn't know where we'd go, but I did know that we had to move while we still could.

As we reached the door of the compound, I looked up at the darkening sky. *Dusk.* Soon the darkness would take over the sky, and the crawlers would be back.

Shutting and locking the door behind us, I headed to

Ozzie's laptop. I swiped at the touchpad and the computer came back to life, out of sleep mode. Ozzie hadn't had time to finish reading the document before we'd gone back out to the hole. Maybe there was something in the document that could help me. Dr. Barrows had been studying the creatures' bones. There had to be some information in there that could help us survive. Fight them.

I skimmed the document frantically, feeling the press of time.

They would be coming back out of their holes soon.

My eyes locked on something and my blood froze.

It is possible that these creatures still thrive in colder areas, like the Arctic.

Differences in bone structure from the glacial bones indicates that the newer bones are a hybrid. They are breeding themselves to be able to withstand a warmer climate.

If that happens, the human race will be annihilated. Wiped out.

I need to find a way to kill them. I need to find someone who can help me. If we don't stop them, then God help us all.

The text ended there, but there were more photos, and the name Griffin Murphy, a Paleontologist at the New York City Museum of Paleontology.

If I could make it to the museum, maybe, together we could find a way. Maybe we could find others who could help us.

I shut the laptop and headed to the couch and sat bundled up in my ski jacket with Hank beside me.

We'd set out at first light, when the lizards skittered back into their holes. We'd be careful of the dirt roads. It would be easier for the crawlers to dig through those. Ozzie or Kyle's pickup truck would make it easier to watch the roads for holes. I'd pack just what we needed, enough food and water to get us to New York City, and UV lights, lots of UV lights. Maybe we'd find help along the way. We could grow our numbers again and be able to fight them off, easier.

With just a little bit of luck, we'd make it. We'd find Griffin Murphy and he'd know how to wipe these things from the Earth.

Maybe they were here first, and they want the Earth back. But we were here last, and I'd find enough of us left to fight them. Expose them to the sun. Kill every one of them.

If our luck held out, the trucks wouldn't be stuck in sink holes and there wouldn't be too many holes around the compound to be able to get out.

Maybe we'd be okay for a while.

Hank placed his head on my leg and I moved a hand over his back, finding comfort in his thick fur.

And we listened as the scratching sounds began.

THE END

INTRUDERS: THE AWAKENING

Zoe's story continues in the second installment of the INTRUDERS series called THE AWAKENING.

Click HERE to check out THE AWAKENING

BECOME AN INTRUDER INSIDER

If you would like to be informed of events happening in the Intruders world, sign up for the Intruders Insider here.

You'll receive information on new releases, promotions, newsletters exclusives, and free stuff.

We value your privacy and will keep your email address guarded like Area 51.

ACKNOWLEDGMENTS

Thanks to my family for cheering me on. Your encouragement means the world to me.

Thanks to Matt Jones, for his wonderful editing work on this book.

Thanks to Yvonne Betancourt, formatter extraordinaire.

Thanks to Ben, light of my life

And, as always, to my husband, Jeff, who is my best friend and strongest supporter. I love you.

ABOUT TRACY SHARP

Tracy Sharp grew up in a small mining town in Northern Ontario, Canada, where there wasn't much to do except dress warmly and write stories to entertain herself. She is fond of horror movies, thrilling novels, bellowing out her favorite songs in the car, iced coffee, flamethrowers and Slinkies. She lives in Upstate NY with her family.

Tracy is the author of three Leah Ryan novels, Repo Chick Blues, Finding Chloe and Dirty Business, as well as the short novel Jacked Up, written with J.A Konrath, the horror novel Soul Trade and a young adult paranormal mystery, Spooked, and the paranormal romantic thriller Flash Fire.

You can visit Tracy at her author page on amazon.

facebook.com/TracySharpBooks

twitter.com/TracySharp

ALSO BY TRACY SHARP

LEAH RYAN THRILLERS

Repo Chick Blues

Finding Chloe

Dirty Business

Red Surf

Jacked Up with J.A Konrath

Spooked

Soul Trade

Flash Fire

AS MELINDA DUCHAMP

FIFTY SHADES OF JEZEBEL AND THE BEANSTALK WITH J.A KONRATH AND ANN VOSS PETERSON

Fifty Shades of Puss and Boots with J.A Konrath and Ann Voss Peterson
Fifty Shades of Goldilocks with J.A Konrath and Ann Voss Peterson

Copyright © 2015 by TRACY SHARP

All rights reserved. No part of this book may be reproduced or transmitted in any form or by any means, electronic or mechanical, including photocopying, recording, or by any information storage and retrieval system, without permission in writing from the publisher.

This book is a work of fiction. Names, characters, places, situations and incidents are the product of the author's imaginations or are used fictitiously. Any resemblance to actual events, locales, or persons, living or dead, is purely coincidental.

❦ Created with Vellum